THE GHOST OF SPRUCE POINT

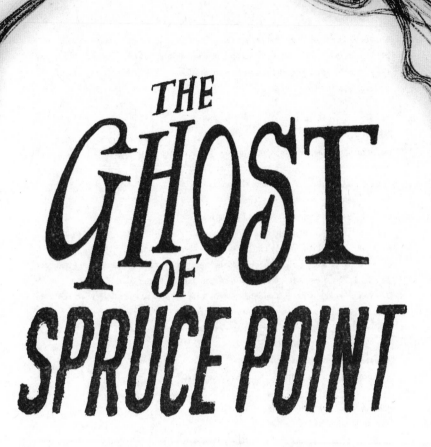

THE GHOST OF SPRUCE POINT

By Nancy Tandon

ALADDIN

NEW YORK LONDON TORONTO SYDNEY NEW DELHI

ALADDIN

An imprint of Simon & Schuster Children's Publishing Division

1230 Avenue of the Americas, New York, New York 10020

First Aladdin hardcover edition August 2022

Text copyright © 2022 by Nancy Tandon

Jacket illustration copyright © 2022 by Kristina Kister

All rights reserved, including the right of reproduction in whole or in part in any form.

ALADDIN and related logo are registered trademarks of Simon & Schuster, Inc.

For information about special discounts for bulk purchases, please contact Simon & Schuster Special Sales at 1-866-506-1949 or business@simonandschuster.com.

The Simon & Schuster Speakers Bureau can bring authors to your live event. For more information or to book an event, contact the Simon & Schuster Speakers Bureau at 1-866-248-3049 or visit our website at www.simonspeakers.com.

Book designed by Tiara Iandiorio

The text of this book was set in Tisa Pro.

Manufactured in the United States of America 0622 FFG

10 9 8 7 6 5 4 3 2 1

Library of Congress Cataloging-in-Publication Data

Names: Tandon, Nancy, author.

Title: The ghost of Spruce Point / by Nancy Tandon.

Description: First Aladdin hardcover edition. | New York : Aladdin, 2022. |

Audience: Ages 8 to 12. | Summary: Twelve-year-old Parker must unravel a curse to save his family's beloved Maine motel.

Identifiers: LCCN 2021060302 (print) | LCCN 2021060303 (ebook) |

ISBN 9781534486119 (hardcover) | ISBN 9781534486133 (ebook)

Subjects: CYAC: Blessing and cursing—Fiction. | Ghosts—Fiction. | Hotels, motels, etc.—Fiction. | Friendship—Fiction. | LCGFT: Ghost stories.

Classification: LCC PZ7.1.T3754 Gh 2022 (print) | LCC PZ7.1.T3754 (ebook) | DDC [Fic]—dc23

LC record available at https://lccn.loc.gov/2021060302

LC ebook record available at https://lccn.loc.gov/2021060303

For Isabelle and Celia

Proof that cousins are
our first friends

Chapter One

ANCHORS AWEIGH

THE BLOODRED MOON casts an eerie glow over the bay. Fog lifts off the ocean and swirls around us as the lapping splash of the incoming tide sways the thick wooden posts of the dock beneath me. If there is a perfect time and place for a ghost story, I'm sitting smack-dab in the middle of it.

"Tell it again, Dad. Please tell it!"

Dad steps back from the telescope and sits next to me, our legs dangling above the dark, churning water. He tightens the hood of his parka against the late-May chill and takes a big sniff of the air. I do the same. If one of the fancy tourist shops in Bar Harbor ever made a candle called Spruce Point, it would smell like this: a mix of spruce, pine, and fir trees layered with the heavy scent of briny ocean.

"You know every detail of this story," Dad says, knocking his shoulder against mine. "You should tell it to me."

"You tell it better," I say. "And Lee Lee's not here, so don't leave out any of the scary parts."

Mom took my sister, Bailey, up to bed already, after they'd had a look at the special moon too. When the moon is full and at its closest to the earth, that's a supermoon. And tonight there's a lunar eclipse too, which makes the moon look red and even cooler. A super blood moon like this only happens once every several years.

I'm the one who tracks all this stuff, and the telescope was my tenth birthday present two years ago. At school, some kids call me Mr. Moon. But not in a mean way. They just know it's my thing. During the school year, Bailey and I ride a van forty-five minutes each way to Bridgewater Consolidated with almost all the other kids who live in tiny towns around this part of Maine. That's pretty much the only time we get to see our friends since it's too far of a drive for our parents to get to any outside-of-school stuff. And even though I miss my friends in the summer, I do not miss that boring van ride.

But luckily, I have one summer friend who makes up for living so far away from everyone: Frankie Wilkins. Every summer since we were six, Frankie's family has rented the cottage right next door to our house, a.k.a. the Home Away Inn, my family's year-round business. I wish she were here to see this right now, but at least she'll be here soon—seventeen days and counting.

A wave rolls in and licks at the bottom of our boots. The tide will be about two feet higher than usual tonight, and that's on top of the already elevated sea level everyone around here is always worried about.

Dad pulls his legs up onto the dock and turns toward me.

"It was a night just like tonight." His voice rumbles low, like he's narrating a movie trailer. "The sailors onboard the *Westward* out of Penobscot Bay knew the coastal route well, and they'd been in worse weather. Spirits were high as the schooner rounded Spruce Point, and the familiar clanging of the floating buoys greeted them."

"The same sounds we hear right now," I point out. I love this part of the story. Completely hidden in the fog, the faint *clang-clung* of the buoys posted off the tip of the point add the perfect soundtrack.

"But then . . . ," says Dad, his voice urgent. I shiver a little, and he puts his arm around me.

"It's chilly," I say. "I'm not scared. Keep going."

Dad clears his throat and continues. "But then

the current swelled, shifting the *Westward* dangerously close to the rocks. The men shouted and ran to their stations, desperate to regain control against a sudden blast of arctic wind. A spark of light, brighter green than anything the men had ever seen occur in nature, flashed across the beach and swelled into a giant orb, which disappeared into the thick forest along the coast. Many believe that in that exact moment, Spruce Point fell under a curse.

"It was certainly true for the crew of the *Westward*. The men were distracted. Confused and momentarily blinded. They had no chance of righting their course, and the schooner was dashed against the rocky shore, the mighty ship reduced to splinters under the force of the rogue waves pummeling the vessel.

"In the morning, villagers mounted a search for the ship's crew that lasted the whole day. While they combed the wreckage, they shared stories about odd experiences the night before. From a chattering flock of sparrows that spun in several tight circles around the church spire before heading out to sea, to a cat who had hissed all night into the empty darkness, each tale hinted that something had spooked the area animals.

"As the sun set, a harsh truth came to light: there were no survivors. All of the sailors had gone to their watery graves, never to be seen again." At this point, Dad always looks down at the ocean and folds his hands for a moment of silence.

"Except . . . ," I whisper after I'd taken a moment too.

"Except, legend says that some nights, when the moon is full, the curse returns and the ghosts of the crew of the *Westward* walk the point, searching for the green light that led to their demise. Their spirits will not rest until the source of the light is revealed. Only then will the link to the curse be broken."

Cool droplets from the fog collect on my eyelashes. I shiver again.

"Dun-dun-dun." Dad grabs my shoulders, leaning me toward the edge of the dock.

I startle, then laugh as a tingle zaps through me. Dad smiles and pulls me to standing.

"Okay, Parker, time to pack up and head inside before Mom sends out a search party." He hoists the heavy telescope, and together we step off the dock onto the pebbly sand, then climb the wooden beach steps toward the inn.

"Wait, Dad," I say, grabbing his arm. "I left my moon journal at the fort this afternoon. Can I go get it? I really want to record this super blood moon. I *need* to."

Dad looks at me with a mix of concern and uncertainty. He knows how much I love things that are predictable, and how amped up and anxious I get when something is left unfinished. Like once when I was little, I had to leave the last part of a puzzle undone because we had to get to an appointment, and I remember feeling itchy and upset the whole time. The way Mom tells it, I was crying so hard by the end that she almost got a speeding ticket driving me home.

I'm working on it, but it's still really hard for me to let things go. *Obsessive tendencies*, the nice counselor at school calls it. I prefer *particular* and *thorough*.

That's one of the reasons I love tracking and charting the phases of the moon. It goes through the same steps, month after month, always reaching toward one of two finish points: new or full. Documenting that predictability helps me feel calm. It's an *anchoring activity*.

"Please, Dad. I have my flashlight. I've been back and forth to the fort a million times, and I know right where I left the journal. I'll be home like five minutes after you."

Dad shifts the heavy telescope and looks from me to the woods to the inn.

"Okay," he says with a sigh. "But straight there and back. And watch your step. Things look different in the dark."

Chapter Two

NIGHT NOISES

I TAKE OFF before he can change his mind. The brownish-red flush of the moon lights the small field of grasses behind our house enough that I have no trouble finding the opening of the path. But a few feet into the woods, I discover that the trail to the fort that I know so well during the day had turned into something completely different after sundown. Bushes scratch at my arms as I shuffle my feet, feeling for the soft yellow evergreen needles I know line the way.

The sounds of scuttling leaves and rustling branches are amplified by the dark, and I switch on my flashlight and swing it in a wide arc, hoping not to see any eyes glistening back at me. I stand still for a moment, letting the slapping waves and the clanging buoys reorient me. Putting the sounds of the ocean to my back, I press deeper into the forest.

Luckily, the trail is well worn from generations of kids going the same way. When Dad was little, he and Aunt Jenny and their friends discovered the old tree house, nearly rotted away by salt air and gusty wind. He said they spent two whole summers replacing boards and rebuilding the structure. When I came along, he made a few more adjustments, saying he didn't want me to have to endure the injuries he had, including countless splinters and a few near-death falls from a no-sided platform. And Mom insisted we install some solar string lights when she did the same around her garden last spring. But after that got all set, it became a place for kids only.

I'm glad now, alone here at night, that I have the twinkling lights as a beacon to head to, and that Dad had insisted on putting in a sturdy ladder. I turn off the flashlight and shove it into my coat pocket so I can pull myself up with both hands. As I climb, chittering noises and the sound of large flapping wings above my head remind me how alive the woods are, no matter the hour.

I crawl onto the platform and notice a dark blob in one of the corners, faintly lit by the swaying lights. I squint and get closer, then crab-scramble backward when I see what it is. A mass of squirming spiders emerging from a golf ball–sized egg sac in the middle of a huge web. Like, hundreds of them, creeping all over each other as they swarm up and over the side of the tree house railing. My heart matches the rapid pace of their wriggling legs.

Snatching my journal, I tuck it into the waistband of my pants and race down the ladder, skipping the last two rungs. I land with a thud and rush back up the path, tripping and stumbling over the roots of the trees looming like dark hulking lumps on either side of the trail. I'm thinking they look a lot more like people than they did on my way in. *Sailors.* I quicken my pace.

When I get to the edge of the clearing and pause to catch my breath, I hear a distinct sound.

Pat, pat, pat.

Footsteps? Maybe Dad came after me to make sure I got home all right.

"Hello?" I call into the darkness. No answer.

Scritch. Swish. Pat, pat.

"Who's there?" My shaky voice disappears into the misty fog that has rolled off the water and is erasing the buildings here on the tip of the point— our home, the cottages, and a few other houses.

As I peer right and left, looking for the source of the sound, I notice something odd about the way the fog gathers and billows in our horrible neighbor Mrs. Gruvlig's yard. It's moving in and out, like her house is breathing. And then, from the tiny slits around the edges of her always-covered windows, a surge of light pushes out into the night. The low cloud of pulsing, dense fog traps and reflects the greenish glow.

The tree limbs behind me lift and wave on a slight breeze, reaching out like arms. I fumble for my flashlight, aim it across the meadow toward home, and run.

Chapter Three

IMPORTANT MISSION

A FEW WEEKS later, the sound of Frankie's whistle, four high-pitched *wheets*, sends me flying to my second-floor bedroom window. The pulley sways and creaks as a plastic bucket travels along the laundry line between us. The Wilkinses got here two days ago, and the thrill of having the whole summer ahead of us nearly makes me dizzy. Or maybe that's just the blood rushing to my head as I lean out to grab Frankie's note.

I open it to see three letters: *K-C-M*. This is the

ultimate code for *I have something exciting and secret to tell you*. I bust into a twitchy wiggle, my insides jittering like I'd guzzled a can of cherry soda. Then I shake out my arms and roll my neck. Frankie says I need to work on my chill.

I scratch *OK* onto the slip of paper and send it back the way it came, calling *cooowah, cooo, coo, coo*. Frankie glances at my answer, then points to the woods behind her cottage. The KCM is *now*. I have to move fast.

"Whoa, hey, where ya headed, mister?" asks Mom, stopping me with her arm as I round through the living room on my way to the back door. She has a cookbook on her lap and is planning this week's menu. People come to the Home Away Inn for two things: the view and the food. At least that's what our online blurb says.

"Outside," I say. *Outside* is the *ultimate code* for getting Mom to let me do what I want. She's powerless against it.

"Oh, good! That's where you kids should

be! But not down by the water right now. Got it, Parker? Wait until the tide goes out a bit." She flicks her fingers through a few snarls in my messy hair and plays whack-a-mole with the piece that pops from the top of my forehead.

"I know, I know. Me and Frankie are just going to the fort, okay?" I duck out of reach.

Before Mom can answer, Bailey comes clumping up from the basement, wearing my pirate costume from last Halloween. The red velvet jacket hangs down to her knees. She lifts the eye patch with one hand and points a plastic sword at me with the other.

"The fort! Can I come?"

"No!"

"Why can't she?" Mom asks. I feel my freedom fading.

"Because Frankie has something to tell me. It's not for little kids."

"Well, that doesn't sound appropriate."

"No, not like that," I stumble. "It's just a KC..." I

suck in the final letter, cringing at my near slipup.

"KC?" asks Bailey. Mom's eyebrows peak.

"Mom, it's nothing bad. I promise. Can I go now?"

"You can if you take Lee Lee. Or you can stay here and tell us all what's going on." No. Breaking the oath is unthinkable.

"*Fine.* Come *on*," I say.

"What's a KC?" asks Bailey again.

I grab her pirate collar and pull her close. "Tell you later," I whisper.

When we get to the back door, Mom calls out, "Whatever you're up to, have fun!"

Yeah, right. Would have been, if Barnacle Bailey hadn't attached herself to my plans.

As soon as we're outside, I hear Frankie's cottage door slam. She comes running into our yard, pulling a bright orange beanie over her short brown curls. She flies right past us to the opening of the trail at the edge of the woods.

"You forgot bug spray!" her stepmom yells from the back porch, the colorful scarf around her neck flapping in the gusty morning wind. "Pull your socks up high! Watch out for ticks! Leave that hat on so hunters can see you! And don't be out too long—it's chilly!"

"I'll be fine, Deb!" yells Frankie, not turning around. "Don't flip, potato chip!"

"It's not even hunting season, Mrs. Wilkins!" says Bailey. "We only have to watch out for bears!"

"She's mostly kidding! We'll be safe!" I call, waving as we hurry to follow Frankie.

As much as my mom loves us playing outside, Mrs. Wilkins hates it. I have no idea how Mr. Wilkins talks her into spending every summer on the coast of Maine. Frankie's dad is a college professor who is writing a book about shore birds, and he says there is no air like salt air for getting the words to flow. But Mrs. Wilkins says she's a city girl who was born for the concrete jungle, not the real thing.

And the truth is, the Spruce Point peninsula is about as far from a city as you can get. Well, unless you count Blythe Harbor, where we do our shopping. It's only three miles by boat to the center of town. Eight if you're biking. Mostly we go to Fairwinds, the grocery store/post office. But we also have Melzen's Feed-n-Seed, the library, and a little breakfast place that changes its name almost every year when somebody new takes it over.

And then there's Swirl Top, which sells the *best* ice cream. They open in early summer, when the first tourists start arriving. That's also when Ms. Pinkerton turns her side shed into the Fish Hut, where she sells seafood. Both places close soon after the swell of people dies down each fall.

All the modern conveniences, claims Mr. Wilkins. *What more could you need?*

Mrs. Wilkins's answer to that is to drive over an hour to Bar Harbor at least once a week, joining the clogged line of loaded cars and huge RVs on Route 3 headed toward Acadia National Park, so she can spend the day among the crowds of visitors poking around the shops in the—air quotes—*big city.*

"C'mon!" Frankie calls over her shoulder. Bailey and I jog to catch up and the three of us fall into a single-file line as we head deeper into the woods. We're all wearing late-spring mud boots. Mine and Bailey's are army-green and already caked with dirt. Frankie's are patterned with dogs and cats holding umbrellas, and she squishes both feet deep into the first big puddle she sees.

Soon the path turns to the left, and the thick evergreens close in behind us. The roaring churn of the ocean fades and the forest settles into a deep, cottony quiet. Safe, alone, we slow down and cross over the plank of wood that Dad put across the tiny brook years ago.

Frankie glances back at me and motions to Bailey with a dip of her head. I shrug my answer.

"It's fine, we might need her," she says.

"Need me for what?" asks Bailey. Frankie doesn't answer. "Guys, need me for what?"

I'm curious too. "Yeah, what's up?" I ask

Frankie, hustling along the path until I'm right next to her. "What's this KCM about?"

"I thought you said it's a *KC*," says Bailey.

"You told her?" asks Frankie.

"No, he *didn't*." Bailey sticks her tongue out at me. "What is it?"

"I sort of slipped up when I was *trying to leave without her*," I say, poking Bailey's shoulder with each word.

"Okay, shhh! I'll explain everything to both of you when we get there." Frankie looks up and down the path. "I don't want anyone else to hear."

We follow the trail as it dips and flows around big, sturdy trees and rotting fallen branches. We push sideways through the pricker bushes. Finally we come to the tree house. Frankie climbs first, then Bailey, then me. Inside, we have an old plastic bin for a table, two round logs perched on their ends for seats, and a carpet of soft yellow-brown pine needles.

"First things first," says Frankie. "Lee Lee, are

you ready to take the oath of the KCM?"

Bailey stands at attention, her fists clenched. "I'm ready!" Then she shifts her eyes between me and Frankie and lowers her voice to a whisper. "But, um, *what is it*?"

"KCM stands for *Kids' Confidential Meeting*," says Frankie.

"*Confidential* means secret," I say. Bailey's smile pulls to the side, like butter slipping off a hot pancake.

"But why do you call it *Kids'*?" asks Bailey. "You should call it *Secret Agents' Confidential Meeting*."

"Bailey, I will forgive that comment because you are new to this," says Frankie. "The KCM is a *tradition* in my family. It was passed down from my cousin Nellie, who is in *college* now. We can't just go changing the name. Got it?"

"Okay, okay. I'm ready. What do I do?"

Frankie raises her right hand and has Bailey do the same.

"Repeat after me," says Frankie. It takes Bailey

three tries to get it perfect, but finally she does:

"I, Bailey Emerton, understand that Kids' Confidential Meetings are for kids only. I will resist growing up with every fiber of my being. This I solemnly swear."

When Frankie nods her head, Bailey bounces on her toes and claps.

"I declare this meeting officially open," I say. "Frankie, what've you got for us?"

"Well . . ." She chews on her lip and pulls at the loose threads of her cutoffs. Frankie's not into made-up drama, so her stall tactics have me ninety-nine percent curious and one percent scared of what she's about to say.

"Listen, here's the deal. I need you to not freak out. And I need you to not get too excited. And I need you to believe me. Swear it."

Bailey raises her right hand again, and I draw my finger in an X across my heart. Frankie peers over the railing, then back at us.

"Okay. Here goes. I saw a ghost in Mrs. Gruvlig's yard last night. A ghost *kid.*"

Chapter Four

EVIDENCE

"**F**OR REAL?" BAILEY squeaks. "You saw a *ghost*?"

"This is huge," I whisper, looking in the direction of Mrs. Gruvlig's. "I've always thought there was something off about that house." I shift from foot to foot in the small space. "*Of course* witchy Gruvlig would have a ghost living with her in that creepy, probably haunted place."

Mrs. Gruvlig is the meanest person I know and one of our only year-round neighbors. She sits in the shady corner of her porch every day staring at the ocean, her little dog Napoleon at her feet, as she picks the meat out of piles of steamed crabs to sell in little plastic containers. Mom tries to wave at her, but whenever Mrs. Gruvlig sees anyone, she tenses her jaw and looks down, shaking her shaggy gray hair so it covers her round weathered face. On Halloween, she's the only person on the whole peninsula who doesn't turn her light on. Probably because she's out on her broomstick.

Mrs. Gruvlig has had a lot of sadness in her life, Parker, Mom always says. But when I ask her like what, she doesn't tell me. *The point is, you never know what someone else's problems might be. It's important to be kind, no matter what.* Mom likes making excuses for grumpy people like that. Her other favorite is *Maybe they have a headache.*

I sit down and pat the boards next to me. "Tell us everything. What did it look like? Was Mrs. Gruvlig with it? Where was it exactly? Did it see you?"

Frankie shivers as she pulls her knees under

her chin. "First off, I couldn't get to sleep last night because this mosquito was torturing me . . ."

"That happened to me once!" says Bailey. "It kept buzzing and buzzing . . ."

"Shh! Let her tell it."

"Anyway, it was late, but I was wide-awake. That's when I heard a weird noise coming from Mrs. Gruvlig's yard."

"Noise?" I ask. It's usually graveyard city over there.

"Yeah. I heard . . . music. Like, someone singing."

"Gruvlig? No way," I say.

"I know, right? So, I got up to check out what was going on, and that's when I saw it."

"It?" asks Bailey. She starts chewing on the cuff of the pirate coat.

"Something small. And human-shaped. Completely white. White hair, white face, and a long white dress or robe or something. It was twirling in and out of the trees, grabbing at the branches, and . . . singing."

"Then what?"

"Then it disappeared. Just, bloop, gone. Right around the back of the house. After that, everything was quiet. Finally I went back to bed."

"Who was it?" I ask.

"This is what I'm saying, Parker. Not a *who*. A *what*. I'm telling you I saw a ghost."

"Did you see any legs?" asks Bailey. "Under the robe thing? Because ghosts don't have legs."

"How would you know?" I ask.

"How would you?" she shoots back.

"Guys. Guys. Focus," says Frankie. "I don't know if I saw legs or not, okay? I was too freaked out."

"Okay, sorry. What else do you remember?"

Frankie folds into a yoga pose, sitting cross-legged with her eyes closed. She rubs her temples. Bailey copies her.

"It was dark," Frankie chants. "The moon was only a sliver. But still, I clearly saw all that white, practically glowing."

"Um-hmm," I say. "Waxing crescent, coming up on a first quarter moon."

Frankie opens her eyes long enough to roll them at me. When she closes them again, she begins to hum. She searches note to note, stringing together a creepy but somewhat familiar tune. When she starts the song over, I join in with the words. "If you go down to the woods alone . . ."

"Stop!" shouts Bailey, hands over her ears. "I don't like that song!"

Frankie puts her arm around Bailey. "Sorry, Lee Lee. Didn't mean to freak you out. You know that song is about having a picnic, right?"

"I know, but I'd never go to a picnic with scary music like that. I don't care how many teddy bears were there."

"Okay, back to last night," I say. "Any other sounds, like chains or moaning?"

Frankie pauses, thinking. "Nothing. And you know what? I never heard Napoleon bark, either. Not once."

"So Mrs. Gruvlig is a witch and her house is haunted?" asks Bailey. "Like, for real, Parker?"

"That's what we're trying to figure out." I turn to Frankie. "There's something else about Gruvlig I've been wanting to tell you."

Bailey scoots closer to Frankie until she's practically sitting on her lap.

"What?" whispers Frankie, leaning in.

"Well, you know how Mrs. Gruvlig almost never has any lights on at night?" I ask.

"She doesn't?" squeaks Bailey.

"Outside or inside," says Frankie. "I've always thought that was strange. When the sun goes down, it's like she disappears."

"Right," I say. "But the night of that super blood moon a few weeks back, I saw a weird glow from behind her closed blinds. And Storm Micah hit the very next day."

"Is that when everything flooded?" Frankie asks. "We saw the pictures on the news even before your dad called us."

"Yeah, it was bad." The N'oreaster hadn't been predicted to come this far north, but it hit us hard and the storm surge had completely washed over the causeway bridge that connects the point to the rest of town. We'd actually been stranded for a few days. A ton of people's basements had flooded, and some boats were lost too.

"After that, I started watching her house more closely. And every time I see a flicker of light from her place, it rains the next day." I lower my voice. "I think the two things are connected."

Bailey tilts her head to the side. "But when Mrs. Rhoades taught us the water cycle, she said it rains because a cloud has gathered enough water droplets."

My hands curl into fists. "I know that, Lee Lee. This is different."

"So a ghost moves in with a lady who seems to be able to control the rain. Something big is going on here," says Frankie.

I nod in agreement.

"FRAN-cis! FRANCIS SOFIA! Where are you? Time to come home!" her stepmom calls from the edge of the woods.

Frankie cringes and punches the floor next to her.

"It's Frankie," she whispers through her teeth. Then she stands and brushes off her shorts. "Ms. Shopaholic insists I need new shoes." I look down at her faded, beat-up sneakers. One of them has duct tape holding the sole onto the toe part. Mrs. Wilkins might be right this time.

"Well, hurry back so we can figure this out," I say.

"Another KCM?" asks Bailey.

"Yeah, but remember . . . ," Frankie says, finger across her lips. "Kids only."

Then we all grab hands, and Frankie and I teach Bailey the goodbye oath.

"Kids' Confidential Meeting—over. Grown-ups—never. Kids—forever."

At the edge of the woods, Frankie turns toward the ocean.

"You know who we need to tell about this," she says, looking across the bay to Fox Island.

"The cousins!" I say, and she grins. "They'll be here soon—Friday's lobster delivery." Then I scrunch my lips and say out of the side of my mouth, "In the meantime, keep a lookout."

Frankie nods sharply and salutes. "You too. Keep your eyes and ears open."

Chapter Five

WORSE THAN A GHOST?

THAT NIGHT I stay up late, camped out on the window seat of my second-floor bedroom, staring at what I can see of Mrs. Gruvlig's dark house. Then I scan the four ocean-facing cottages that people can rent from us. There's a light on at Frankie's, to my left, between us and Gruvlig's. The three others, to my right, sit empty and silent. I don't see any signs of anything living (or not) moving around. I do hear something that scares me, though.

Below me is our front porch, where Mom and Dad sit most evenings, wrapped in thick blankets. Usually their quiet voices mix with the night noises in a soothing way that helps me fall asleep. But this time they're talking at a level somewhere between discussion and argument. I press my ear to the screen.

"We can't keep going like this," says Dad.

"I don't understand," says Mom. "Three summers ago, we had a waitlist ten-people-deep. Remember? Every night, all the rooms and cottages full. Swirl Top had to pay Henry Sullivan to wear that orange safety vest and direct traffic in and out of their parking lot. The whole town was rich with tourists!"

"Yeah, and how about that time Melzen's sold out of all their fishing gear? Those two guys from Portland almost got into a fistfight over the last deep-sea rod. . . ." Dad chuckles.

"See, that's what I don't get. Is no one interested in secluded peace and quiet anymore? Is it all theme parks and big splashy hotels?"

"Well, there's a difference between *secluded* and *isolated*. The way climate change is playing with the coastline around here is no joke. The higher this sea-level rise gets, the more times that causeway is gonna be underwater and impass-able. I think people from away get nervous about being stuck out here."

Mom lets out a whoosh of air. "I suppose you're right. And you know our tiny town will be last in line for any help from the state. Not with all the other places being affected, too. That new bypass on Route Three isn't helping either. Acadia traffic skirts right around Blythe Harbor now, instead of coming through. Which keeps Spruce Point even more hidden."

"Everybody's feeling the pinch," Dad says with a sigh. "I saw Macy Pinkerton in town today, and she said she might not open the Fish Hut this year."

"You're kidding! She's already thinking that?"

"Yeah, partly because her stitching group was

talking about how many relatives are putting off visits because of that weird brown-tail-moth infestation. Apparently the little hairs they shed are toxic! I guess her nephew had quite a reaction after he was climbing in her trees and disturbed some nests. Poor kid was covered in a rash and had a horrible asthma attack. Even had to go up to the hospital in Bangor for treatment."

"Oh, how awful. They're the ones that are all white except for the one brown strip, right? Those buggers are certainly doing a number on all the oak trees around here. The leaves are stripped, like it's winter!"

"And without the leaves to change color, we'll lose some shoulder-season leaf peepers too. Seems like everything is working against us," Dad sighs.

"But worst of all," says Mom, "is when we do get people to come all the way out here, they have to deal with Mrs. Gruvlig's stink eye watching them the whole time. It's zoned for a hotel, for heaven's sake! We showed her all the paperwork. Should we try talking to her again?"

Dad grunts, and I imagine him shaking his head. There is silence for a moment, but not the peaceful kind.

Finally Dad says, "All I know is, we can't afford for this place not to make a profit. We used up all our savings getting it back into shape. We're maxed out, honey. Honestly, unless things turn around and we fill up soon, this might have to be our last summer on Spruce Point."

"Don't say that! I mean, I know things have been a little slow—"

"A little slow? We haven't been at capacity in two years!" says Dad.

"Okay, but what else would we even do?" asks Mom. "Our whole lives are up here now. And it's not like there's anywhere close by where we might get work."

"I could always become a lumberjack. I'm pretty good with an ax."

This makes Mom laugh, but the ha-ha part fades right away, like a candle being blown out.

"Seriously, hon," says Dad, his voice quieter now. "There's always teaching. I'm still in touch with almost everyone from my old school. Boston's not so bad. You could call up the bank, see if there are any openings . . ."

"Absolutely not," says Mom. "How can I spend my days in a fluorescent cubicle after this?" Her voice shifts into cry mode, breaking the last word in half. Dad's footsteps creak across the porch.

"Look, I'm not saying definitely, I'm saying maybe."

"It's only June," Mom sniffs. "There's still time to think of something. Right? We'll think of something?"

"We'll have to," says Dad.

I crawl down off the seat and into bed, where I lie on my side, arms around my knees. Dad always talks about how he and Mom took over the inn and the four cottages from Nana the same year that they chose me to be their son. He calls it his double lucky year.

One of my favorite pictures is Mom holding two-month-old baby me in front of the hazelnut tree Dad planted the week they brought me home. *The minute we saw you, we knew you were meant to be rooted right here with us*, Dad likes to say. The Home Away Inn is the only home I've ever known. This is my place, with my tree. And I want to stay right here, where I belong, forever.

Then I realize something that makes me curl into an even tighter ball. *Keep your eyes and ears open*, Frankie had said. Could what's going on at Mrs. Gruvlig's be part of the reason the inn wasn't doing well? I knew there had been some arguing between her and my parents about the use of the point as a vacation rental spot. Dad had assured me we had all the proper permits and things from the town. *We're in the right*, he'd said. But Gruvlig basically hates people and would probably love it if we left and took all the tourist traffic with us.

And if she couldn't push us out legally, would she look for a more menacing way to get us off the property?

I'd been tracking her spark-fests along with the moon phases in my journal. And I hadn't made up that every time I saw a flash from her house, it was followed by rain. Which is probably the ideal environment for moths. And now she's conjured a *ghost*, too, something that would surely scare guests away. It all leads to one conclusion. There has been a resurgence of the Spruce Point curse. And witchy Mrs. Gruvlig is behind the whole thing.

Chapter Six

COUSIN ALERT

ON FRIDAY MORNING, Bailey's voice pierces through the entire house as she lets out a scream.

"Ghost??" I say, sitting up fast and hitting my head on the low, angled ceiling. Heart racing, I peek into the hallway.

"They're here! They're here!" cries Bailey. A flash of forest green whizzes across the landing. Even though her tights are ripped and her hat has no feather, I can tell she's Peter Pan today.

"Here, here, here, here, here!" Bailey crashes down the steps and into Mom, who is standing at the bottom with flour-covered hands and a wrinkled forehead.

"What in the world?"

"Cousin alert!" Bailey sings. Mom claps her hands and sends bits of white dust flying.

"Oh, good! Parker, come on down. We'll need your help."

Relieved, I slip on a sweatshirt and head out to the dock. Every Friday in season, my aunt Jenny delivers lobsters and mussels she's caught and harvested. She never moved away from Spruce Point like Dad did. She simply sailed across the bay and set up on Fox Island. And when Nana tried to give the inn and property to both her and Dad, she wasn't interested. *I've got my camp and my kids and my boat and the ocean*, she always says. *That's all I need.*

As the sturdy *Adah Ruth* putts closer, my cousins Sylvie and Drake lean through the side windows, waving and shouting. The second the boat bumpers hit the dock, they both jump out and pull the ropes tight, securing them to the cleats. When you grow up homeschooled on an island, you learn how to tie up a boat before you learn to tie your shoes.

"Parker! What's up?" Drake reaches to give me a high five with a chocolate-smudged hand. His wind-blown hair makes him look like a red fox that fell into a cotton-candy machine.

Bailey takes Sylvie's hands and twirls her around and around, nearly stepping off into the water. Sylvie's neat braids fling out as the girls spin, her long skirt lifting to reveal tall rain boots.

"Careful!" says Aunt Jenny. She grabs Mom's outstretched hand and steps onto the dock too. "Special delivery!" she says, pointing to the boxes in the back of the boat. Lobster is always the main course for Mom's annual *Welcome Summer* dinner, which she'll serve tomorrow night for the Wilkinses, the only guests so far.

"Hop to it, kids," says Mom, "and when you're done, the biscuits will be ready. C'mon, Jenny, I've got a fresh pot on." They head up to the house arm-in-arm. Aunt Jenny is Dad's sister, but she and Mom act like they grew up together too.

I'm about to complain about unloading all the stuff when I remember Mom and Dad's conversation from last night. Maybe if I do more work around the inn, that would help us stay open. I know it's probably not as simple as that, but at least I'd be doing something.

Bailey flops onto her belly and splashes her hands in the water.

"Hey," I say. "We *all* have to help bring these up."

"You're not the boss of me," Bailey complains.

I could go into my whole *I'm your older brother, I'm always the boss* speech, but I don't want to argue. I'm too anxious about letting the cousins in on the fact that a ghost has moved in next door.

"I want to finish this quick, so we can head to the fort," I say. "For a you-know-what."

"Ohhhh!" says Bailey. "Do these guys know about . . ." She holds her hand up in oath-swearing position.

"Yup. You're the last KCM-er," I say.

"KCM?" Drake smiles and flutters his fingertips together.

"We've got something to tell you," I whisper, glancing over my shoulder at Dad, who is setting up to fix one of the loose dock boards.

"Frankie get here yet?" asks Sylvie.

"Yup."

"Better send a signal."

We unload the boat in record time.

The cousins have known Frankie as long as Bailey and I have, and we all get really excited for her visits. The four of us are it for kids our age around here. And our parents don't believe in spending money to send us to camp, since we basically live in one.

So, Frankie is our one-kid version of summer camp friends, and the five of us hang out together all the time. But me and Frankie are the only ones who have a special handshake. It started a few years ago as a rock-paper-scissors over who would get the last piece of gum. When I kept winning, it stretched from the best two out of three to the best five out of six, and then Frankie started adding stuff she called "style points." She made me follow along with *hands on hips* and *elbow to elbow* and *head-shoulders-knees-toes-pop*. And that's how we got the Frankenparker. Things are always more fun with Frankie. From the moment I met her, I felt like I'd been tied to a bunch of helium balloons—lighter, ready for adventure. We ended up splitting that piece of gum.

Thank goodness she's back at the perfect time to help me figure out all that's going on. As soon as we're done putting the boxes into the walk-in cooler at the back of the kitchen, I grab a biscuit and head up to my room, where I scratch a note for Frankie.

KCM – Cousins here – P.

I slip the code inside the bucket and pull on the clothesline to send it over. *Cooowah, cooo, coo, coo,* I call. There's no answer. I have to bang the bucket against the window frame a few times before Frankie lifts open her screen and grabs the paper. She glances at it, gives me a thumbs-up, and disappears.

I run back to the kitchen for another biscuit and the rest of the bacon.

"Hey, that's too much!" says Bailey. "Leave some for us!"

"There is no such thing as too much bacon, Lee Lee." But I do hand her one of the strips.

I turn to the cousins. "Hey guys, finish up. I wanna show you the changes we've made to the fort." I look straight at Sylvie and spell out *K-C-M* in sign language. We taught ourselves the whole alphabet last year out of a book from the library. She stuffs in her last bite and takes her plate to the sink.

"Let's go!" she says.

"Don't stay out there too long," says Aunt Jenny. "I've got two trees to take down today." The cousins are always splitting logs into firewood for their woodstove, no matter what time of year it is.

"Aw, we just got here!" says Drake.

"They can hang around with us today, if you'd like," says Mom. "Paul can run them back tonight on the skiff." It doesn't take much to talk Dad into a boat ride, especially after a long day of working on the property.

"Yes! Please?" asks Sylvie.

"Well, if you promise to help out if you're needed, and don't get in the way."

"We promise!" shouts Drake, bursting out the

door before Aunt Jenny can say anything else. We all follow right behind.

Frankie is already waiting on the porch for us.

"Frankie!" shouts Drake, running around her in circles. Sylvie gives her a sideways hug.

"KCM!" Frankie yells, and we take off running. The early-morning fog is still floating among the spruces and pines. It gathers us in, erasing the rest of the world. The only thing visible is the trail beneath our feet, and we leap over logs and swirl through ferns like we were forest-born, shouting into the misty freedom. We climb up and squeeze into the fort, taking big gulps of air into our burning lungs.

Sylvie recovers first. "What's the big news?"

"Frankie saw a ghost!" blurts Bailey.

"Seriously?" asks Drake. He had been unwrapping a lollipop, but his hands stop, frozen.

"Okay, hold up. There's no such thing. What are you even talking about?" asks Sylvie, her arms crossed.

Frankie explains all that we know so far.

"Are you sure you saw it go around the back of the house? It didn't disappear into the ground?" asks Drake, gnawing on his thumbnail.

"Pretty sure," Frankie says. "Why?"

"Because . . ." Drake stops and looks over at Bailey.

Bailey sticks her chin out. "Yeah, why?"

"Well, what if Mrs. Gruvlig has a body buried in her yard, and this is its ghost?"

At that exact moment, a hawk swoops over the tree house with a loud screech.

"AHHHHH!" yells Bailey, throwing her arms around me.

"Okay, okay, calm down. Don't be such a baby," I say. But I pull her a little closer instead of pushing her off. "I'm sure there isn't a dead body over there."

"Are you?" asks Frankie. She makes a *woo* noise.

"Right? Aren't ghosts basically dead bodies?" asks Drake.

"No," peeps Bailey. "A ghost is totally different from a dead body."

"Oh my gosh. Shush, all of you!" says Sylvie. "I'm sure you saw something, Frankie, but I'm also sure there is a reasonable explanation. When was this? Two nights ago?"

"Yeah. I watched last night too but didn't see anything," says Frankie. "You, Parker?"

"No, nothing."

Frankie taps her lips. "Although I did figure out the exact spot on my porch where I can see the whole side of Gruvlig's house, and anything going in or out the front and back doors. It's the perfect place for a Stoop Snoop."

"What's that?" asks Drake.

"It's something my friends and I back home do all the time. We sit on our front steps and make it look like we're minding our own business, when really we're keeping track of everyone else's," says Frankie. "But this one's gonna have to be at night, when ghosts move around."

"Ghost patrol!" Drake raises his hand. "I volunteer!" Frankie gives him a high five.

"You guys *have* to sleep over!" says Bailey, pulling on Sylvie's shirt.

"Agree, we need to be here for this," says Sylvie. "Mostly so I can keep you all from completely losing it."

"Excellent. What else?" I ask. I open our supply bin and pull out a pocket-size notebook and pencil. The other kids call out ideas and I write them down.

GHOST PATROL
binoculars
dark clothes
sleeping bags
flashlights
notebook/pencil
drinks
snacks

The plan is set. Now all we need to do is figure out a way to keep Sylvie and Drake here overnight, then wait for it to get dark.

"Parker," asks Bailey on our way back up the path. "What will we do if we see the ghost?"

Good question.

Chapter Seven

DRIFTWOOD

WE TALK THE parents into letting Sylvie and Drake sleep over tonight by promising to help in the garden this afternoon. Mom is an amazing cook, and according to her, the inn's food tastes so good because almost everything she serves comes from our own garden, the ocean, or farms right here on the peninsula.

Drake and Bailey are on weed duty, and Sylvie and I are hilling up the potato plants. Frankie helps us, even though she doesn't have to. Mom sprinkles fertilizer onto the dirt between her rows of lettuce, asparagus, and beets.

"It's been such a wet June," says Mom, swatting away a black fly. "I'm worried these plants will never take off. How will I make my almost-famous Green Supreme smoothies for our guests, then?"

"You could always just get what you need at the store," I say. "Right?" The knot of worry I've been carrying around since the other night pulls tighter.

"Well, I *could*," says Mom. "But that's not how we do it around here. Serving food fresh from this garden is one of the things that sets us apart, and we really need to be highlighting what we have that no one else can offer. But I might end up having to buy some supplies, because look at this . . ." She waves her hand over the puny sprouts. "What we've got here would barely make a side salad."

My mind flicks to one word: *cursed.*

"Can Drake and I go down by the water now, Mom?" asks Bailey. "These flies are so annoying!"

Mom looks toward the rocky beach. "Hmm . . . low tide . . . okay. If one of the older kids goes too."

"Me!" Sylvie quickly peels off her gloves.

"Take the bucket and shovel and get some clams while you're down there," says Mom. "I'll clean them up and give them to Mrs. Wilkins to thank her for hosting your sleepover tonight."

Drake starts to giggle, and Bailey joins in.

"What's so funny?" asks Mom.

"Nothing," says Sylvie, shaking her head. "C'mon, let's go!"

When they're gone, Mom turns to me and Frankie. "I have to go make some phone calls. Can you two finish up here without me?" Her eyebrows pinch together, creating a deep wrinkle.

"Sure," I say, misting more bug spray on my arms. "We're almost done anyway."

Mom gives my shoulder a squeeze, then walks back toward the inn.

"What's up?" Frankie looks at me through squinted eyes.

"What do you mean?" I work the dirt into rounded piles up around the potato plants.

"You never do work without complaining! Something's up. Spill."

I stand to stretch my back and look around the yard. The gray cottages with freshly painted white decks, Mr. Wilkins's station wagon, the cool shade of the trees, the big three-story Home Away, even Mrs. Gruvlig's dark house . . . It's all so familiar and special to me.

I close my eyes, and the churning ocean fills my head. I hear little white waves bouncing off the tiny islands that dot the bay. I smell the seaweed-draped rocks on the shore, warm now from the sun.

When I open my eyes again, Frankie is staring at me, her trowel hovering in midair. "Parker?"

I almost don't want to say it out loud, even though I know ignoring what I heard won't make it less true. But this isn't a problem that can be fixed by a group of kids meeting in a fort. And

I'm not sure someone who has a life away from here will be able to understand why the thought of leaving this place is so painful to me.

But Frankie's not just someone. She stands up and puts her hands on her hips, mouth set in a straight line. She's already gearing up, ready to take my side against whatever's bothering me.

"The inn is in trouble. And I think we might have to leave if we don't have a good season this year."

Frankie's mouth drops open. "What?"

I tell her everything I overheard.

She looks around and shakes her head. "Not. Okay."

"I know." I lift my shovel up and slam it down into the dirt. "But what can I do?"

"*We're* gonna do something. Okay? We'll do whatever it takes to make sure this is the absolute best season the Home Away Inn has ever had."

"Like what?" I ask, my voice cracking in an embarrassing squeak. "How is anything us kids can do going to fix something this big?"

"Well, first, Mr. Half-Empty, you need to give me a second to think about it. There're probably a million ways we could help! We'll figure it out."

Just then Mrs. Gruvlig scuttles across her side yard. She runs her hand across the pieces of driftwood hanging from a branch of her beech tree. They knock together, creating an eerie, hollow sound that blows toward us on the wind. Then she turns sharply and disappears into her basement through the cellar door.

"Hey, Frankie? Do you think there is such a thing as curses, like for real?" I ask.

"You mean, like actually harnessing some kind of power to make something bad happen to someone?"

"Yeah, someone or some*place* . . ."

"Oh, like that story your dad tells about the green light and the drowned sailors?"

"Exactly," I say. "And what if that story isn't just a story? And now, generations later, what if the force behind the green glow has gotten into the wrong hands somehow, and the origins of that curse have been rekindled . . ."

I motion with my eyes toward Mrs. Gruvlig, who has come back up, cradling something in her arms. We watch her weave a length of gauzy fabric loosely around the hanging driftwood. Then she pulls what looks like a swatch of dark wool from the pocket of her long sweater and fixes it to the gauze with a thin pointy stick.

At that moment, Frankie slaps her hand hard against a spot on her neck where a black fly had landed and gone in for a bite. Her palm comes away with a smear of blood, and her eyes go wide.

"Think about it," I continue. "After all these years, why are my parents now suddenly having trouble keeping the inn going?" I ask.

Frankie takes a step closer to me. "You think it might be cursed." She says it like a statement, without a hint of teasing. She flits her eyes toward Gruvlig.

"Or even this whole peninsula. I don't know." I kick the heel of one boot against the toe of the other, releasing a clod of dirt. "Never mind. I get how weird that sounds."

"Hey, *weird* is my favorite." Frankie looks once more at Gruvlig, then leans in so our foreheads are practically touching. "Look, I think there's a *lot* of supernatural stuff going on all the time that we don't know about, because people get too hung up on reality. Luckily, we're not those people. We'll look for evidence tonight. Anything's possible."

The way Frankie uses the word *we'll* gives a helium-balloon lightness to what moments ago had felt so heavy. I'm not alone. Maybe together we really will be able to find some way to help the inn, starting with figuring out what's going on next door and how we can stop it.

"Let's hurry up so we can get down to the beach too," I say, slamming my shovel into the dirt.

"Now, that's the Parker I know," says Frankie.

Chapter Eight

PERIWINKLES

W E CLAMBER OVER beach rocks as the sun burns a watery hole in the sky. Bailey and Drake roll up their pant legs.

"Ready? Go!" says Bailey. The two of them wade in up to their knees, grunting and squealing.

"So. Cold." Drake grits his teeth and flaps his arms.

"It hurts!" says Bailey.

"You should give up, then."

"You first!"

They stomp their feet as the icy water attacks their winter-white skin, turning it bright pink. Finally Bailey runs to shore, yelling, "Surrender!"

We all poke around the pebbly sand, looking for treasures. Frankie finds a hunk of blue sea glass still in the shape of a bottle neck.

"Beginner's luck!" I say.

"You say that every year!" She gives me a shove.

"You guys, come here!" shouts Drake. We follow his voice around the bend, where the bay tucks into a cove near the causeway bridge. The receding tide laps gently against its concrete retaining wall.

Drake's kneeling at the edge of a tide pool. "Look at this." He points to a large, neat circle of small yellow periwinkle shells.

"A fairy ring!" shouts Bailey, reaching back to pet the gauzy wings she's wearing today.

"No it's not," I say. "No such thing."

"Oh, but there *are* ghosts?" Sylvie asks.

"Whatever," I say.

"Guys. There's both," says Frankie. She leans in to inspect the shells. "Anyway, no way these ended up like this on their own. Someone arranged them on purpose."

I slip the small notebook from the fort out of my pocket, open to a fresh page, and write *Clues* at the top of it. "I'm gonna write this down," I say. "In case it might make sense later."

CLUES
Ring of shells

As I'm writing, the others scramble up and stretch out on top of one of our favorite boulders, exposed by the receding tide. When I join them, I push into a spot next to Frankie, sighing as I sink onto the warmth of the wide rock's sun-bleached top.

After a while, Drake sits up to dangle his legs over the edge. He pops a hunk of gum into his mouth.

"I can't believe this is your backyard," says Frankie, joining him. She tosses a stone into the water. "You all are *so* lucky. Back home, it's already so sticky hot you can barely breathe. And the heat makes my street stink like warm garbage all the time—way worse than low tide, trust me!" She shades her eyes and scans the horizon. "I'd love to stay here forever."

Her words snag a memory I haven't thought of in a while. *Forever.* When I was four, Mom and Dad sat me down and read me a book called *My Family Is Forever*, and for the first time told me straight out the story of my adoption. I was snuggled between the two of them on their bed, and I remember thinking that *forever* meant listening to the ocean while I was surrounded by warmth and love. This place is tied to my story—it's where I started my life a second time.

"Guys, there's something I need to tell you," I say.

Frankie nods at me.

"Hmm. MMM!" says Drake, pointing to his huge bubble. I watch it stretch until it's almost see-through.

"I don't know how much longer we'll be here," I blurt out. Drake's bubble pops and deflates down his chin like a pink beard.

"*What?*" asks Sylvie.

"Parker, are you teasing me?" asks Bailey.

"I wish I were, Lee Lee. I heard Mom and Dad talking about going back to their old jobs if the rooms and cottages don't fill up this summer."

"That can't happen," says Drake.

"It won't," says Frankie. "I already promised Parker. We're going to think of something. Some way to help."

"Count me in," says Sylvie. "You guys can't leave us here alone! But I will say, my mom's been really worried lately too. I guess absolutely everything's been slow this season. She's definitely getting fewer orders and selling lobsters way cheaper than usual."

"Go ahead, tell them the other thing too," Frankie says to me. "The *real* reason the inn might be in trouble."

"You mean besides not having enough guests?" asks Sylvie.

"Right," I say. "Things have been slow, but why? Think about it. Who's the one person who would love for us to leave?" I look over my shoulder in the direction of the houses.

"Gruvlig!" says Drake. I nod and lean in, motioning them all to come closer.

"The evidence is growing. Mrs. Gruvlig is a witch. And I think she's reawakened the curse on Spruce Point that took down the *Westward* all those years ago," I whisper.

"Parker . . . ," says Sylvie, shaking her head. "That's only an old story!"

But Bailey's and Drake's wide eyes stay focused on me, and Frankie motions for me to keep going.

"Hear me out." I point at the sky. "The rainiest June ever, including one huge storm that actually flooded the road." I look at the causeway, then continue counting off on my fingers. "The horrible garden so far. Only one cabin booked. Those awful brown-tail-moths. I mean, toxic hairs? What's up with that? Plus . . . well, you all know what Frankie saw." I spread my hand. That's five things.

"*Allegedly* saw," says Sylvie.

"But let's say it's true," Frankie answers. "And if it is, tell me, what kind of a person would have a ghost at their house?"

"The witch kind," whispers Bailey.

"Exactly," I say. "And I'm thinking Gruvlig brought the ghost here as part of the curse—to scare even more guests away!"

Drake presses his fingers into his forehead, rubbing small circles. "Oh man. This is wild. *Wild!*" He pulls his gum out in a string. "Okay, so, what do we do now? How do you break a curse?"

"Not sure," I admit. "I mean, obviously for starters, we need to figure out who or what this ghost is. I think that's the key. Gruvlig's never going to talk to us. But this ghost might give us clues to how we can get her to stop what she's doing."

Sylvie clears her throat. "How about for starters, we come back to reality and think of what we can do to *actually* help the inn?"

"You're both right," says Frankie. "We do need to investigate the ghost. But in the meantime, we also have to think of some way to make a lot of people want to come here. Or a way to raise a bunch of money, fast."

It's quiet while we watch a group of small sailboats from a nearby camp tack their way across the reach.

"Did you think of anything yet?" asks Bailey, tapping her finger on Frankie's knee.

"Not yet," Frankie says, giving her hand a squeeze. "But we will."

"And don't tell Mom and Dad about any of this," I say, pointing at Bailey. "They have enough to worry about."

"I *won't*." She tosses a pebble at my feet.

Soon we hear the familiar clanging of the bell that hangs on our back porch.

"Dinner!" says Drake, sliding down the rock and racing up the beach.

"See you after, at my place," says Frankie. "We've got work to do!"

Chapter Nine

GHOST PATROL

AFTER DINNER, WE all meet on Frankie's porch to set up our *Stoop Snoop*. Frankie balances the binoculars with one hand and feeds herself a slow and steady stream of cheese puffs with the other. She was right about this being the best spot. In the dusky light, we can see the whole side of Gruvlig's house through the sparse growth at the bottom of the hemlocks along the property line.

"So, what exactly do we do on ghost patrol?"

asks Bailey, hopping on two feet up and down the Wilkinses' front steps.

"Shhh!" I say. "You don't say *ghost patrol* out loud!"

"Fine. What do we do *now*?" she whispers.

"We look for clues," I say, surveying the yard through a rolled-up piece of paper.

"Like what?" Drake digs a piece of hard candy out of the snack bag.

"Like anything out of the ordinary," says Frankie. But Gruvlig's house looks exactly the same as it always does. Plain brown wood siding. Windows with the shades drawn. No lights on, no signs of life.

"Why *is* it always so dark over there?" asks Frankie.

"Maybe she only uses candles. Or she lives in the basement," says Sylvie.

"Or she has night vision, like an owl," I say.

"No, she uses echolocation, like a bat!" Drake curls a hand behind his ear.

"That's totally it," I say. "She turns into a bat at night. Wait, no . . . that's vampires. Anyway, she's a witch-bat, and that's why she wears that long raincoat-cape thing of hers so much! She has wings folded up under there!" I grab my shoulders and flap my elbows.

"I would totally love to see that," says Frankie. "Wings would be cool!"

"And Frankie Wilkins was *never seen again*," I say in an ominous reporter's voice. Then I lean into the darkness, my eyes slowly scanning along the side of Gruvlig's house. Scrubby plants, wood siding, dry grass, tree trunk, and . . . wait.

"What is *that*?"

I motion for the binoculars, snapping my fingers.

"What?" says Frankie, standing up and handing them over.

I find the back corner of the house and then scan left to right until I see it again. There! Five rocks, stacked one on top of the next, biggest to smallest. "It's like one of those rock thingies that people build on hiking trails. Was that always there?"

I point Frankie's head in the right direction.

"Oh! I see it!" she says. "I don't know. I think that might be new. Everybody look."

We pass the binoculars down the line. "I'm pretty sure that's called a *cairn*," says Sylvie. Everyone agrees it's the first time they've seen anything like this in Mrs. Gruvlig's yard.

"Another clue!" says Drake, taking out the notebook. On the *Clues* page, he writes *Rock tower*.

"Let's go see it up close," says Frankie. "Maybe there's more to it than we can see from here."

We clump together and sneak into the yard on soft feet. Curving my hands to hide the glow, I flick on the flashlight and we inspect the cairn. The rocks are ordinary, except for how they're stacked. I move the guarded beam around the nearby area and stop it on something even more interesting. I motion for the others to have a look.

It's periwinkle shells and sea glass. Arranged in a circle.

"Just like the one at the beach," whispers Drake.

The only difference is that one has a scallop shell the size of my hand in the middle, its two big domed sides still hinged together.

The sudden clattering sound of dishes sends us all scuttling to hide. Frankie guides the younger two back into her yard where they squat next to her dad's car. Sylvie and I are together behind a round compost bin.

"Eww . . . ," Sylvie whispers.

"It's not that bad for compost," I say. I've smelled worse.

"No," she says, pointing. "Look."

I follow her finger and see a faint, pulsing glow through the slats of the blinds in a downstairs window. On the outside, the glass is covered with moths. Their dark gray bodies are huge and speckled, so I don't think they're the venomous kind. But seeing so many all together is still creepy. The light from inside glimmers again.

"That's the weird flashing I've been talking about!" I whisper.

"That's just her TV flickering, Parker. But those moths do seem to be drawn to it." Sylvie shudders. "Let's get out of here!"

I hear Frankie whisper-call *wheet wheet wheet wheet*, and the five of us gather on her porch again.

"Drake, hand me the notebook," she says. "Something's arranging those shells. And I want to send them a note. What should we say?"

"You guys, no," says Sylvie. "This is silly."

"How about, *Are you a ghost?*" asks Drake, ignoring his sister.

"*How come we never see you in the daytime?*" says Bailey.

"*Is the curse a real thing?*" I add.

"Hang on. So many questions right up front feels kind of rude, like we might scare it off. Let me concentrate a second," Frankie says. She closes her eyes and makes little chanting noises, swaying her head side to side.

I can't help it. I snort a laugh.

"Parker! This is serious!" she says. I try to control my lips from smiling.

Frankie's eyes snap open. "I've got it!"

She turns to a fresh page. I shine my flashlight so she can see. She leans over the paper and speaks out loud as she writes.

Ghostly Spirit: We come in peace
and ask you to break the curse.

Then Frankie tears out the note, folds it, and slips off the porch back toward Gruvlig's.

"Hurry!" I whisper.

She comes back, breathless and smiling.

"Where'd you put it?" asks Bailey.

"Inside the scallop shell. Right in the middle of that ring."

"You guys are going to be very disappointed,"

says Sylvie. "There's nothing over there. No one's going to get that note."

"We'll see," says Frankie. "I have a hunch. No harm testing my theory."

"Never a dull moment with you, Frankie." Sylvie smiles. "And I guess we're not hurting anyone, so . . ." She shrugs and goes to her sleeping bag.

Frankie and I keep watching through the hemlocks, but the glow from the window is gone. Soon the inky blackness of cloud-covered night sky blots out our ability to see anything beyond the Wilkinses' porch.

Bailey yawns, and she and Drake pull their sleeping bags right next to each other and turn on a solar lantern to read. Drake has one of my comic books. Bailey is looking at a book about animals, as usual.

"A *troop* is a group of monkeys," she says as she pokes her head out of her bag.

"What?" asks Frankie.

"That's what you call a group of monkeys. A

troop. This book tells you all different kinds of names like that."

"Hmm," says Frankie.

"And a group of gnats is called a *cloud* and group of butterflies is called a *kaleidoscope*," Bailey continues.

"Okay, give it a rest, Lee Lee!" I snap. "You're going to scare the ghost away!"

"*Ghost?*" asks Mrs. Wilkins, who has come out to say good night.

"He's kidding, Deb. We were just telling ghost stories," says Frankie.

"Okay, but not too scary, all right? And anytime anyone wants to come inside where it's warm and dry and civilized, you're more than welcome."

"We're fine, Mrs. Wilkins, thanks," I say.

"It's called camping *out*, not camping *in*!" says Frankie.

When she leaves, Frankie and I wiggle into our sleeping bags next to Sylvie. I lie on my belly and prop up on my elbows, staring through the binoculars at the blank, black space between us and Gruvlig's house.

"So, tell us about life in civilization, Frankie," says Sylvie. "Don't leave anything out." Sylvie always talks about going away when she grows up, to a big city where no one knows her and everything's new. No thanks. Not me. I like things right here, exactly the way they are.

The girls whisper back and forth while I keep watch. Soon, all is quiet.

It's getting chilly. And besides the mosquitoes, I think I'm probably the only one still awake on the whole peninsula.

Sometime later, the sound of the binoculars hitting the porch floor startles me awake. As I jerk my head, a dim flicker of green pulsing light near the back corner of Gruvlig's house catches my eye. Before I can fully focus, the flash swoops right at me. I try to reach over to wake Frankie, but everything feels fuzzy. I'm out of my bag and off the porch, the light pulling, pulling me past

Gruvlig's and out toward the woods. My legs are numb, not working, and yet I'm still moving forward. The light has surrounded me now, the greenish vapor pushing against my face. I open my mouth to try to call to the others, but the mist seeps in, choking my words. I'm almost to the edge of the woods when I feel a sharp thump between my shoulder blades.

"Parker! Parker, wake up!" Someone's slapping my back and pulling on my arm.

I gasp and gulp for air. Frankie's face comes into focus and I reach for her hand. Partly to get her to stop hitting me, and partly to see if she's real.

"Did you see that? What happened?" I ask, my mouth dry.

"I woke up and you were gone! Then I heard a horrible choking noise and saw you all the way over here out in the field! What are you doing? Are you okay?"

I scan the blackness of the yard. There's no

haze or mist or light around me. I'm standing near the woods in my pajamas. This makes no sense. "I . . . saw something."

"Where? What?" asks Frankie.

I try to describe it, and she tries to believe me. It's cold, so we head back to our sleeping bags and spend the next half hour staring at unmoving shapes in the darkness and listening to insects and other familiar night noises.

"I think you had a dream, Parker, and you were sleepwalking," Frankie finally says with a yawn. "Let's talk more about it in the morning." Soon her head drops to her pillow and she begins breathing slow and heavy.

After a while, I slip into a restless sleep, where this time I dream my home is balanced on a shifting pile of rocks that one by one keep disappearing.

Chapter Ten

LOOK UP

A REPETITIVE, HARSH sound wakes me.

Caw-caw-caw. Caw-caw-caw.

I open my eyes and follow the sound to a large black crow perched on a dead branch of the biggest tree in Mrs. Gruvlig's yard. He won't shut up. The same three squawks, over and over, like he thinks he's a rooster or something.

"Ugh, quiet!" I say, pulling my pillow over my head. It's a drizzly, cool, Maine-in-June morning, the sky a dome of gray above us. Rain coming the day after I see lights at Gruvlig's tracks with my earlier observations. I'll have to record this in my journal. But right now my body feels stiff, and my sleeping bag is snug and dry. I burrow deeper.

Then I hear a loud fluttering of wings. It sounds like someone is flapping the pages of a giant book. When I peek out again, a whole flock of crows is covering Gruvlig's lawn.

"Look at that," says Frankie. She's on the porch steps, a big wool sweater pulled down over her knees. "Have you ever seen so many in one place before? You can't even see the ground!"

It's true. There must be fifty crows. They're noisy and restless. We all peel out of our bags.

"Migrating home?" I ask.

"Maybe," says Sylvie through a yawn. "Some crows do migrate." She hugs herself tight and rubs her arms.

"Um, Parker?" says Bailey.

"Just a minute," I say, staring at the crows.

"Or they could be on their way to Branch Lake

for fresh water," says Drake. He's balancing on one foot and pulling a thick sock onto the other.

"Parker!" says Bailey.

"But such a huge group," I say, ignoring her. "Look at 'em all!"

"Guys, listen to me!" Bailey claps her animal book shut with a thud. We all turn. She holds the book to her chest, then leans in and lowers her voice. "A group of crows is called a *murder*."

The screen door bangs open and I jump. The crows are startled too, and they rise together like a loud, dark puff of smoke, disappearing over the water. Only that one pesky crow stays, crying out over and over.

"Good morning, campers," says Mr. Wilkins. He sits on the top step with Frankie, clutching a steaming mug. "Ah, the *Corvus brachyrhynchos*, a majestic yet annoying feathered friend.

"Did you know scientists think crows actually have their own language and can recognize faces?" he asks. "Apparently, they can really hold a grudge, too. Seems like that one might have a bone to pick with your neighbor there."

"And a group of crows is called a *murder*," says Bailey. "I learned that in this book."

"Hmm . . . ," says Mr. Wilkins, sipping his coffee. "A murder."

"What on earth are you telling these kids?" asks Mrs. Wilkins. She hip-bumps through the screen door, bringing a box of Pop-Tarts out to us. The Wilkinses have the best breakfast food.

"Only sharing a bit of ornithological knowledge, my dear," he says. Then he stands and pats Frankie's head. "But now I'm off to the office." He grins and heads inside.

We each grab a foil packet and follow Mrs. Wilkins back into the kitchen, because it's too chilly to stay outside.

"What are you kids up to today?" she asks, pouring orange juice for each of us. Her long, sparkly fingernails catch Bailey's eye as she sets down our glasses.

"We should play nail salon!" Bailey says.

"No thanks!" says Drake. "Anyway, I know what I'm doing. Swirl Top opens today, and I'm so there!"

"Yes! Let's all go!" says Frankie. "Can we, Deb?"

"Maybe after lunch, if this rain lets up. Make sure you check with the other moms first, though." She hoists her giant pocketbook onto her shoulder and buttons her sweater all the way to the top. "As for me, I'm headed into town to see if I can get some cell service and use the library's Wi-Fi. I swear the connection gets worse out here every year. I'm completely out of touch with the real world!"

"Okay," says Frankie. "Have fun looking at all your friends' very important vacation pictures." Mrs. Wilkins puts a hand on her hip and purses her lips but then blows a kiss.

After breakfast, we go back to the porch to gather our stuff. That's when Frankie and I tell the other kids about my odd experience last night.

"Spooky," says Drake. "I wish I hadn't slept through that!"

The lone crow flaps to the peak of Gruvlig's house and resumes his squawking. I'll bet Mrs. Gruvlig put one of his buddies in a potion or something.

Bailey looks over in that direction, then says, "That's weird."

"What?" I ask.

"The rock thing. It got taller."

At lunch, we convince Mom that Sylvie and Drake need to sleep over for a second night.

"We can do whatever chores you need," says Sylvie.

"Yeah! Anything! I'll taste all your recipes!" says Drake.

"Well, aren't you sweet," says Mom, like she knows we're up to something. "I really could use the help, though. Since we have space, I opened up the dining room to people from town, and a couple of families have called to say they're coming! It'll be like old times—a full house for our *Welcome Summer* feast. I'll call and let your mom know I'm keeping you another night."

"Yes!" says Sylvie. Drake gets up and runs around the table a few times before crashing back into his chair.

The drizzle stops while we're having lunch, so Mom agrees to our plan to ride to Swirl Top after. When we're finished eating, we head to the shed to dust off our bikes. A few tires need air, and then we're ready to go. Sylvie uses Mom's bike, and I use Dad's so Drake can use mine. We meet up with Frankie and pedal along Wilder Road as it curves around Blythe Bay, taking us into town. At Swirl Top, there's a bunch of people out front who have waited all winter for this day, same as us. We balance our bikes against the side of the building and get in line.

I already know I'm getting a large vanilla twirl dipped in cherry, so I don't need to look at the menu board. The predictability of opening day, and knowing they'll have my favorite summer-only treat, adds to the calm I'm feeling. Under the take-out windows, I see a few flyers advertising stuff like the library book sale happening next week, and the first of the *Thursdays on the Lawn* concerts, which happen in July outside the church. Later in the season the whole wall will be covered, but for now there's space. That gives me an idea.

After we order, I pay for all of us with the money Mom gave me. "Can I hang something on the front wall here later?" I ask the girl in the window as she hands over my change.

"Sure thing, bud. Knock yourself out."

I join the other kids on the grass and bite the tip off my cherry shell, slurping the first slightly melted sip of cool sweet vanilla through the opening. "Guess what? The cashier said we can put up an ad for the inn right here. If at least ten people from away see it, we could be full by July first!"

"That's an awesome idea," says Frankie. "I'll help. I've got this cool art set. Do you have any big paper?"

"We could use the back of my science fair poster," says Bailey. "My rock candy never grew anyway."

"Perfect," says Sylvie. "Let's go back and get started. Meet ya at the fort!"

We finish off our cones and grab our bikes for the winding ride home. The sun peeks out, and I unzip my jacket and tie it around my waist. As we race up the lane, the wind lifts the hair off my forehead, and the smell of fresh balsam and salt-water rushes past. If there is a curse on Spruce Point, I can't feel it today. All I feel is hopeful.

Chapter Eleven

GHOSTLY GIGGLES

BACK AT THE fort, we lay the poster board on top of our supply bin and start planning the ad. Frankie wasn't kidding about her art set being cool. When she opened the wooden box, the sides each lifted two more times until it was three levels high.

"How about if I do a sketch of the tip of the point down in this corner," she asks, "so the words can be front and center?"

"Good idea," says Sylvie. "You start on that."

"I'm gonna go get a bunch of pine needles we can glue on to make it 3D," says Drake. Bailey wants to put glitter on the whole thing.

While Sylvie and I brainstorm words that come to mind when we think of the inn, I use the tip of a stick to poke at the delicate webbing holding the empty egg sacs that the spider volcano erupted from the night of the supermoon. I peel the whole torn web off our railing and fling it over the side of the fort. At least it was spiders and not those venomous moths. My arms itch just thinking about the stinging rash that sent that kid to the hospital.

"Hey, what about something like *Spruce Point* being the *high point* of a vacation?" Sylvie asks.

"Ooh, I like that." Frankie moves to the side so we can lay out stencils for the words.

"Wow!" I whisper. With a sharpened colored pencil, Frankie's flicking individual blades of seagrass onto an incredibly realistic drawing of the tip of the peninsula.

She flashes me a smile. "Mondays at the Met—*Landscapes with Master Neal Tworkin*."

"Huh?"

"It's this thing Deb signed me up for last winter at the art museum. It was that or ballet." I smirk, picturing Frankie in a tutu. "She likes me to 'take advantage of the city's cultural richness.'"

"You're really good!" says Sylvie. "Oh, I wish we had classes like that around here. We have *no* culture."

"Hey, we had that owl-drawing thing at the library that one time," says Drake, coming back with his hands full of white pine needle clumps.

"Okay, my art class was fun," agrees Frankie. "But it's like Deb is allergic to downtime. She's obsessed with enrichment. I mean, did she *have* to sign me up for piano this year too, just because the guy who tunes the Steinway for the Philharmonic had an opening? And that's all on top of swim team! I swear I feel like I can't breathe sometimes." She throws her head back and takes an exaggerated sniff of the air. "There. Enriched. Now let's finish this poster."

Sylvie and I carefully trace the letters. *Make Spruce Point the high point of your vacation—come home to the Home Away Inn!* We let Bailey put glitter on the exclamation point while Drake glues pine needles on the four corners.

When Mom rings the bell for us to come help with dinner, we hold up our work to have a look. It's pretty good. The stencils and Frankie's drawing make it look almost professional. But the glue isn't quite dry, and the needle clumps keep shifting. So after we close all the craft supplies and our notebook back into the bin, I lay the poster down flat on top of it and start fussing to fix them back into place as the others climb down the ladder.

"Should we carry this back with us so we can add more?" I ask over the edge of the platform.

Frankie's head pops back up through the opening. "It's fine. It's done. Leave it here to dry."

I press one more time on a pine bundle in the

bottom left corner. The bell rings again. Frankie slides the rest of the way down the ladder and waits until she sees my feet before starting down the trail.

"See you at dinner!" she calls, heading home to change.

Mom puts Sylvie and me to work scrubbing mussels. Drake and Bailey are on table-setting duty. Dad is hanging a string of small white lights, and Mom whistles as she dances around the kitchen.

"A full dining room tonight!" she sings.

"No one can resist your cooking, oh great Queen of Cuisine," says Dad, pinching the edge off a warm roll and bowing low. Mom swats his hand with a dish towel.

"Leave some for the guests!"

"Yeah, I sure hope there's enough," says Dad, surveying the mountains of mussels, lobsters, potatoes, and corn heaped in steaming serving trays. There are plenty of other dishes too, like crabby mac-n-cheese, and spicy pickled green beans that we canned at the end of last year. Mom always cooks enough for an inn full of guests. The recipes were inherited from Nana too, and Mom doesn't like to change anything about them. Apparently including the serving size.

The bells on the front door jangle, and Mom takes off her apron.

"Showtime!" she says.

Mom and Dad hug Mr. and Mrs. Wilkins and shake hands with the people from town. Pastor Taylor's here with his grown-up daughter who visits every summer. They sit down with Helen and Elvie, the two older ladies who run the yarn shop, which is only open "by chance or appointment." Frankie joins us at the kids' table. Dad takes drink orders and fills our glasses with sparkling grape juice.

"A toast!" he says. "To summer!"

"Hear, hear!" says Mr. Wilkins. "To summer on Spruce Point!"

I take a quick sip of my juice to push down the lump forming in my throat.

"Let's eat!" announces Mom.

We dig into the feast. I help Frankie attack her lobster, cracking up as bits of shell go flying. "I can't believe you forget every year how to do this," I tease her.

"Hey, if you ever come visit me in the city, we'll see how good you are at figuring out the subway system," she says. "Besides, this way you do all the work and all I have to do is eat."

I shake the claw I'm holding in her face.

"Sarah, you absolutely must share this recipe with me," says Mrs. Wilkins, closing her eyes as she bites into the mac-n-cheese. "Carbs and dairy never tasted so decadent!"

"Good luck," says Pastor Taylor. "I begged the senior Mrs. Emerton to let us include her recipe in the church cookbook for years, but she never would part with it!"

"I'll bet we could figure it out," Miss Helen

teases, and Elvie nods. She takes a bite. "I know I taste nutmeg."

That starts a friendly argument about the contents of the dish, and whether it was an Emerton original or stolen from Lennie Richardson, the wife of the first minister over on Deer Isle. This is how grown-ups entertain themselves around here.

After dinner, we clear the tables while Mom serves dessert to the guests. Then she lets us each take thick pieces of Come Again cake out to the porch.

"I love the *Welcome Summer* feast," says Frankie, licking the last crumb of fudgy chocolate off her fork.

"Me too," says Drake, letting out a big burp.

"Ewww!" says Bailey.

"Excuse you," says Sylvie.

"Shhh!" says Frankie. "Did you hear that?"

"That burp? Who didn't?" I say.

"No, I swear I just heard a giggle."

"A giggle?" asks Bailey.

"From over there," says Frankie, pointing. "You guys didn't hear that laugh?"

We all go silent and scan the yard for movement. But we don't see or hear anything else. The waxing gibbous moon, a few days past the quarter, is like a dim night-light and not much help.

"Did it sound like a ghost?" I whisper.

"Was it a cackle?" Drake presses against my side.

"I don't know," says Frankie. "But I know I heard something."

All the hair on my skin stands at prickled attention.

Before we can investigate further, the town guests leave, and Mr. and Mrs. Wilkins come out onto the porch to gather Frankie and say goodbye. We beg for another sleepover, but Mrs. Wilkins says not tonight. Mom agrees and shoos us all off to get into pajamas.

Drake and I lie head-to-foot in my small bed. He's holding up one of my comic books, and something on the back catches my eye. It's an ad for a web series that promises to teach you how to cook like a professional chef. Only $19.99.

"Can I see that?" I ask, grabbing the comic.

"Heyyy!"

"Look," I show him. "If people will pay twenty bucks to watch a video to learn how to cook, how much do you think they'd pay for a lesson from a live person?"

"I don't know. I don't like to cook. I only like to eat."

"Not you, Drake. Like, people from town, and tourists. Guests are always asking my mom for her recipes. I wonder if they'd pay her to teach them?"

"Oh!" says Drake, catching on. "I guess. But I'm not sticking around to do the dishes."

I lift my leg out from under the blanket and shove my smelly sock in his face. He grabs my foot and starts tickling. Soon we're laughing so hard that Dad hears from downstairs and booms, "Boys, settle down!"

"Yeah, boys," calls Bailey from her room across the hall, where she and Sylvie are side by side on her trundle bed.

"Who asked you?" I yell.

"I did," says Sylvie in a fake low voice, and the girls start to laugh then too.

When Mom calls up a few minutes later to tell us to *quiet down I mean it*, that's all we need to completely lose it. It's the kind of laughing now that tips into pain, because your gut hurts and you can't get your breath. Then as soon as you do, you laugh some more.

When I finally start to drift off to sleep, my lips keep twitching into a smile. And the last thought I remember having is how weird it is that I can hear an echo of our laughter from far away, somewhere outside my bedroom window.

Chapter Twelve

SOMETHING HAS BEEN HERE

A LIGHT, PERSISTENT tapping wakes me up. At first I think it's Bailey, knocking on my door to annoy me. But when I open my eyes, I see that my bedroom window is sleek with water. It's a medium rain, the kind that Mom would say is good for the garden, if the garden soil wasn't already soaked. I shift slowly, untangling my legs from Drake's arms, and watch the droplets swell and then race down the glass. My mind wanders to all the things Mom might ask us to do if we're stuck inside today. She'll never let us ride to Swirl Top with our ad if this keeps up.

Swirl Top! The poster! Of all the cool features we've added to the fort, a rainproof roof is not one of them. Even though the poster is probably ruined by now, I swing my legs over the edge of the bed and pull on my jeans and sneakers. Then I hurry downstairs and grab my raincoat from its hook by the back door.

My sleepy legs jolt awake when the cold rain hits them. I jog down the trail, careful not to slip on the mossy rocks. Inside the tree house, I'm expecting to see a soggy, glittery mess. But instead, I see . . . nothing. I inspect the area, thinking the wind probably blew the sign away. But it's nowhere. Maybe Frankie came and got the poster last night, if she heard it was going to rain?

Then I notice a little white triangle peeking out of the supply bin. I open it up, and there's our poster, nice and dry. Classic Frankie. I should have known she'd have my back. Last year when I had to do four packets of summer math, Frankie sat with me every morning, helping me break up the work into chunks so that I could get to a finish point every day.

"How come you're helping me with this?" I'd asked her. She told me, "My dad says *a problem divided is a problem conquered.* Plus, it's more fun to do stuff when you're around, anyway." So yeah, she's that kind of friend.

Now I carefully tuck the poster inside my coat and head back home. The rain is slowing down, and when I get to the little bridge, for a minute I stand still and pretend I'm the king of this misty forest. I hear the scurrying feet of a little critter, probably a chipmunk, and imagine an army of them lining up to bow to me. I drink in the rich, wet earth smell and try to imagine what it would be like to be Frankie, and to have to wait all year for this.

I tilt my head to look up into the tops of the trees and see something I hadn't noticed before. Dozens of weird gauzy nests. They're not on every tree, but some have them on multiple branches. I back away slowly, worried they belong to brown-tailed moths. But when my head bumps the leaves, a whole big group of gray moths lifts off. *No white, no brown, no problem*, I think, until I see that they are coming right at me. I step backward, swatting them away from my face. But then more launch, and they all join together, the cloudy blur of their little bodies and fluttering wings filling the space around me until they begin to lift higher and higher. I watch in awe as they blot out my view of the sky overhead before the mass shifts and they seem to peel off one by one, disappearing again into the thick foliage.

I shudder and move quickly on shaky legs down the rest of the trail and out into the field, where I look up at my home. It's quiet and dim, except for one kitchen window with a warm yellow glow. Mom's looking out of it, and I take a deep breath and try to slow my racing heart. Then a sharp *snap* to my right jolts it again.

Mrs. Gruvlig is in her front yard, dressed in her long black rain poncho with the hood up. She's picking up sticks and thin branches, breaking them into smaller lengths before putting them into a barrel. When she sees me, her mouth twists into a tight frown. Then she holds out a larger branch and cracks it in two with a swift kick. In the tree above her is that one loud crow, screeching over and over like an alarm.

Shivering, I hurry up the porch steps. I shake some of the rain from my jacket and kick off my sneakers before going inside.

"What're you doing up so early?" Mom asks, helping me out of my coat.

"Saving this." I hold out the poster. "But Frankie beat me to it."

Mom takes the sign from me and sets it on the table. Then she sits down with her coffee and studies our creation.

"This is fantastic! I love the wording—*Make Spruce Point the high point*—how clever."

"Thanks. Sylvie thought of that."

"What made you kids think to do this?" asks Mom, fingering the edges.

I walk over to the cupboard and get a mug and a packet of hot chocolate mix. *Kid coffee,* Mom calls it. Allowed on cold, wet mornings. I'm stalling, trying to decide if I should come clean about listening in on her and Dad's conversation. I decide to go for the half-truth.

"I got the idea looking at all the ads posted on the wall at Swirl Top."

"Well, you're a smart kid. Because we sure could use more guests—this year, especially."

"Why especially?" I ask, trying her out.

"It's nothing for you to worry about, but we've had a few light years in a row, that's all. I'd love to see the old ship running at full steam again, you know? And to be able to dust off that 'No Vacancies' sign!"

"Well, I hope this poster helps," I say, blowing at some loose glitter.

"I'm sure it will," says Mom, but she whispers it. She stands and goes back to the window, tracing her finger in looping swirls on the condensation, something Bailey might do. The rain has stopped.

"Hey, Mom, do you know anything about cooking classes?"

"Why, you looking for a new hobby?" Mom grins and I smile at her.

"I meant I was wondering if you've ever thought about teaching one. I saw an ad in a comic book. Did you know people will pay money to learn how to cook?"

"Oh, I don't know, honey—I'm not a professional. I'm sure those classes are taught by people who have training, and degrees, stuff like that."

"Well, you're the best chef *I* know," I say.

"Couldn't agree more!" says Dad, coming into the kitchen. He runs a hand through his wild hair and gives Mom and me each a kiss on our foreheads. "What are you two *cooking up*?"

"Parker wants me to offer a cooking class. Can you imagine?"

"Actually, I can imagine that very clearly, Sarah," says Dad, pouring coffee.

"You boys can't be serious," she says. But her eyes sparkle.

"People are always asking you for the inn's recipes," I say.

"*Sarah's Home Away Cooking School.*" Dad arches his hands over an imaginary sign. "I like it."

"Hmm," says Mom. Then she turns to her shelf of cookbooks, humming and tapping a beat along their spines.

Dad winks at me. I slurp the last of my cocoa and grab the poster. Time to kick off the plan to save the inn.

Chapter Thirteen

WHO OR WHAT

U P IN MY room, I slide open my window and haul back the bucket. Drake moans at the blast of cold air and snuggles deeper in the blanket. I write out a quick note for Frankie.

Thanks for saving the poster!

Hand over hand, I pull on the laundry line until the bucket bumps against Frankie's window, whistling *cooowah, cooo, coo, coo*. She lifts her curtain and waves. I flop onto my beanbag chair and wait for her response. Soon the bucket comes back to me. *Wheet wheet wheet wheet,* calls Frankie.

I reach in for her reply.

1) "Saving the poster"??
2) KCM after breakfast—I have news.

That's weird. If she didn't put the poster in the supply bin, who did? Maybe Sylvie. I'll ask her about it when she wakes up.

I go back to the kitchen to get some breakfast. Mom is putting a loaf of blueberry bread in the oven.

"Hey, can you hang around here and take this out when the timer goes off?" she asks. "I want to go putter in the garden while the rain has stopped. Dad's gone to the Feed-n-Seed and will be back in a bit."

"Sure." I pull up a stool and flip through the notepad next to the phone until I get to a blank page. First, I think of a good name for our plan. Then I list what I've thought of so far.

OPERATION INN KEEPERS: OINK
1. Break curse (??)
2. Advertise (poster) and get more guests
3. Cooking class—Mom
4. ??

When the smell of the bread reaches the other kids, they come downstairs. We each cut big hunks, and Sylvie pours us all glasses of milk. We're almost done eating when Mom comes back inside.

"Mornin', sleepyheads. What's the plan for today?"

"Swirl Top!" shouts Drake, spitting bits of bread from his mouth.

"I don't think so," says Mom. "You were just there yesterday!"

"But we *have* to go, to hang the poster," I say, wiggling my eyebrows at Drake.

"How convenient," says Mom, catching my look and sending me a wink.

There's a loud clanking on the front porch, and the door swings open.

"Bailey!" hollers Dad. "How many times have I told you to put the clam bucket and trowel away properly when you're done?"

Bailey turns toward him, fastening the top button of her Red Riding Hood cape. "I did!" she yells.

Dad comes into the kitchen and holds out the bucket and rake. "Oh really?"

"Really," says Drake. "I was with her! We put that stuff up on the shelf in the shed where it goes. I remember!"

"Then why did I find these things on the front porch?" asks Dad.

"I don't know! It wasn't me!" says Bailey. Dad looks unconvinced.

"Let's not worry about who did or didn't do

what. Please help put them away now," says Mom in her end-of-discussion voice.

Bailey grabs the stuff and heads outside. I smirk at her back.

But then Dad says, "And you three look like you might need something to do too. I happen to have picked up a half dozen bags of manure for the garden this morning that need unloading."

"No, Uncle Paul!" says Sylvie, wrinkling her nose. "It's too gross!"

"You won't be saying that when you're biting into one of Aunt Sarah's triple-decker tomato sandwiches later this summer!" he says.

Just then, Frankie appears at our back door, knocking K-C-M in Morse code.

"Sorry, Dad, we're busy!" I say, tearing off my *plan* and shoving it into my pocket. "Frankie needs us!"

We dash outside before he can ask any questions and race to the fort, calling for Bailey to join us.

When we get there, Frankie ties her raincoat around her waist and points at me.

"Parker, you go first. What were you saying about the poster?"

"I came out here this morning to rescue it from the rain, but it was already tucked in the supply bin. I thought you'd taken care of it last night."

"No, wasn't me. Did you do it, Sylvie?"

"Huh? Don't know anything about it." She raises her hands in surrender.

"Bailey? Drake? Did either of you come out here since yesterday?" I ask. They both shake their heads.

"That's strange," says Frankie. "And let me tell you my news too. I saw something last night." Her face is serious, eyes bright.

"The ghost?" whispers Bailey.

"Here we go again," says Sylvie.

"I know you're the resident skeptic and all that, Sylvie," Frankie says, "but I definitely saw something I can't explain."

"What happened?" I ask, glancing over my shoulder.

"It was super early this morning. The rain woke me up. I like to sleep with my window open, you know?" Frankie is always talking about how much she loves the sounds and smells of the point. "So, I got up to close it, and I swear to you, I saw this small . . . figure, draped in like a long dark coat, but way too small to be Gruvlig. It was walking around near the path to the beach steps, dragging a shovel. Then literally I blinked and it wasn't there anymore. Blinked!"

"It was going to bury something!" whispers Drake.

"Maybe," says Frankie, shivering. "I stood at the window and watched for a long time, but I never saw it come back."

"It wasn't just someone going down to the beach?" asks Sylvie. "People do get up wicked early around here."

"In the rain? That early? I don't know. And it

was small, like a kid. And all the kids I know of on Spruce Point are sitting right here." Frankie pats the worn floorboards in front of us.

"Did anyone else see anything this morning?" asks Drake.

"I saw something kind of weird," I say. Everyone turns toward me, and my shoulders give an involuntary shake. "I was coming out of the woods, and a whole group of moths practically dive-bombed my head. It was gross."

"We should be recording all this stuff as possible clues," Drake says. He takes the piece of red licorice he's holding and pretends to write with it in the air.

I nod. "Definitely."

Drake pops the licorice into his mouth and pulls our notebook out of the bin. But a moment after he opens it, he throws it onto the floor like it's hot, pointing at it and sputtering, "Ah. Uh. Urgh."

"What're you doing?" Frankie asks. She leans

over to pick up the book and looks at what he saw. She sucks in her breath and lets it right back out with a yell, jumping up and down.

"What's going on?" asks Sylvie.

Frankie holds up the page for us all to see. "IT. WROTE. BACK."

Chapter Fourteen

EASY MONEY

T HE WRITING IS messy, like maybe it had
been written in a rush.

> Sorry I have no idea about a curse.
> But I'd like to learn more. Maybe I
> could help? Let's meet. Pick a time
> and place (not daytime). Somewhere
> dark. I'll try to be there.
>
> —AG

"AG?" asks Drake. "Ooh, I bet that stands for A Ghost!"

We all stare at each other in shock and silence. Sylvie's mouth opens and closes a few times.

I slowly take the notebook from Frankie's hands and turn back to the *Clues* page. My hand shakes a bit as I add to the list.

CLUES
Ring of shells
Rock tower
Poster was moved
Figure with shovel
GHOST NOTE

"Parker?" Bailey asks in a small voice. "Is this real or pretend?"

I look to Sylvie. I almost want her to say something like *This can't be happening* or *No such thing.*

But instead she says, "There's no way Drake

and I are leaving now; we *have* to spend the night again. We need to find out who wrote that note!"

"Duh!" says Drake. "That's what we've been doing all along—trying to figure out who the ghost is!"

I find my voice. "They want to *help*? But they don't know anything about the curse? This makes no sense."

"Let's write back right away," says Frankie. "And find out more." She looks at the note again.

The clanging bell sounds, calling us to lunch. I shake my head. "We can't go now! This is too important!"

"We have to," says Drake. "It will look suspicious otherwise. Also, I'm hungry."

"Drake's right," says Frankie. "Let's all go up and act natural. But in the meantime, everyone be thinking about how we should respond. And get ready for another sleep out, because tonight we're back on ghost patrol!"

Mom has stuff laid out for us to make our own

sandwiches and is washing vegetables in the sink when we get to the kitchen.

"Frankie, there's plenty, please help yourself," Mom says over her shoulder. "And everybody take at least one carrot stick!"

"Thanks!" says Frankie, heading straight for the jar of Mom's homemade pickles.

We quickly make our food and talk about everything *but* the note as we eat. Mom dries her hands and joins us at the table.

"How's it going, team?" Mom asks after a bite of a turkey wrap. "Did you have a fun morning?"

"Good!" says Bailey.

"Yes!" I add.

"Nothing!" says Drake. I see Sylvie flick his leg under the table.

But Mom doesn't notice. She has something on her mind. "Were you guys planning to ride over to Swirl Top to hang your poster today?"

"Yeah," I say. "We'll go as soon as we're done here, if that's okay?"

"Sure. And . . . um . . . put something else up for me, too?" She wipes her hands on a napkin, then goes to pull a piece of paper out of the printer tray.

She comes back and puts it in the middle of the table. "What do you think?"

In bright blue across the top, it says: *Sarah's Home Away Cooking School*. Underneath is a list of some class titles, like *Decadent Desserts* and *Seafood Soups & Chowders*. It also shows dates and times and our phone number.

"Mom! You're doing it!" I say. "Look, you guys, people are gonna pay for Mom to teach them how to cook stuff!"

"I hope so," says Mom. "I'll stop by the library later to update our website, but I figured old-fashioned advertising would be a good idea too. I don't know—I guess we'll see if anyone is interested."

"They will be. I know it," says Sylvie. "If you weren't my aunt and already teaching me stuff, I'd sign up!" Then she lowers her eyes with a sigh and adds, "I wish we could stay over *one more night* so I could cook dinner with you again. I learn so much when I'm in the kitchen with you!"

"Well," Mom says, her hand waving off the compliment. "I'm sure your mom won't mind sharing you a bit longer."

Later, with the flyer tucked in my pocket, and the poster curled under Frankie's arm, we all take off on our bikes toward town. The air is humid, and I'm sweating when we get there. We ditch our bikes under a tree near Swirl Top's parking lot, and Bailey and Drake head to the swings on the small playground in the side yard.

Frankie, Sylvie, and I stand back to see where the best spot to put the ads might be. Finally we agree on a space to the left, where we'll only cut off the very bottom corner of a *Bean Supper, Saturday 5:00 p.m.* announcement. I pry out some old thumbtacks and we hang the signs.

"Hey, look at this!" Frankie says, pointing to a

bright orange construction-paper pumpkin.

"*Plan now! Bring your biggest and best home-grown produce to the fall Peninsula Fair*," Sylvie reads. "*New categories: weirdest potato, tiniest tomato, and curliest string bean. Back by popular demand: largest pumpkin—$500 cash prize.*"

"Right, they do that every year," I say.

"Five. Hundred. Dollars?" squeals Frankie. "For a pumpkin? Awesome!"

"Yeah, it's no use trying, though," says Sylvie. "Mr. Haight wins every year."

"It's true," I agree. "It's a thing."

"Oh c'mon, you should enter, Parker! Your parents have that huge garden—I'm sure there's space for you to plant some seeds. And you could use the prize money to help the inn!" says Frankie.

I picture my parents' smiling faces as I hand over a big wad of cash. I know it wouldn't be near enough. But at least it's something I could do, right now, to try to help. It's better than sitting around worrying.

"Okay, worth a shot," I say. Frankie claps her hands. "I'll put it on the OInk list."

"The what?" asks Sylvie.

"Operation Inn Keepers. Check it out." I pull the plan out of my pocket and unfold the paper. "This is everything I've thought of so far." While the girls look it over, I get a pencil from the check-out window to update the list:

OPERATION INN KEEPERS: OInK
1. Break curse (??)
2. Advertise (poster) and
get more guests
3. Cooking class—Mom
4. ?? Win pumpkin prize money

Then I run to the playground and belly-flop onto a swing. It soars forward with my weight, and I spread out my arms. That's how big my pumpkin is going to be. Wing tip to wing tip. Big enough to finally knock old Mr. Haight from his throne.

On the way home, I peel off from the other kids to stop by the Feed-n-Seed. I ask Mr. Melzen which seeds grow the biggest pumpkins.

"Ah, ya got yuh eye on that contest, do ya?" he asks.

"Maybe."

"A little late to staht, better use this quick-growin' kind," he says, pushing a packet of seeds called *Atlantic Prizewinner* across the counter to me. Then he gives me a bunch of advice about exactly how to grow them. I must look confused because finally he taps the packet and says, "Follow what it says on the back. Good luck to ya, boy."

Dad is still in the garden when I get home, so I tell him my idea, minus the part about giving the money to him and Mom. I want that to be a surprise.

"I need a big spot, because Mr. Melzen said a prizewinning pumpkin will take up a lot of space."

"You're welcome to that area," Dad says,

pointing to a churned-up patch next to the main garden. "But it's gonna be all on you, you're in charge. I've got my own stuff to focus on."

The dirt is loose and easy from all the rain, and I work in a bag of compost and form three hills. Then I poke some holes, drop a seed in each, and water them. I run my finger over the simple directions outlined on the back of the packet. I've never thought about it before, but growing things has a predictability to it too. I'm feeling really good about this new gardening gig. The packet says they should sprout in five to seven days, and to thin them down to one plant per hill a week later. After that, I'll let Mother Nature take over.

Easy money.

Chapter Fifteen

WRITING BACK

AFTER DINNER, WE gather at Frankie's to set up our next ghost patrol. It's time to focus on our note and what we're going to say back.

"Okay, all clear," Frankie whispers into the darkness. We're on her front porch, our sleeping bags in a circle. A minute ago, Mr. Wilkins did his final check-in and clicked off the living room light, which had been sending a yellow glow across the floorboards. Now the brightness of the full moon takes over. Streaks of blue and dark shadows surround us.

We sit up in our bags, and Drake passes around gummy worms like he's dealing cards. I shine my flashlight on the note we got at the fort.

"What we say next is really important," Frankie says. "Hang on, I'll get a candle. It'll feel more official if we write it by candlelight."

She goes inside and comes back with one of the big, scented ones Mrs. Wilkins keeps on the mantel, and the fireplace click lighter.

We all sit around the lit candle and Frankie takes the pen and notebook.

The woods rattle with a slight breeze, and a whisper of the fishy smell of low tide passes through.

"It says for us to pick where we should meet." Frankie taps her finger on the word *place*. "But that'll be tricky. The parents are never going to let all five of us go off together after dark."

"Except," Sylvie says, "to watch the Fourth of July fireworks."

Frankie rewards her with a punch. "Ohmygosh, that's it! We can meet up during the fireworks while everyone else is watching the sky. And that's not too far off—great idea!"

"So glad I thought of it," Sylvie says, rubbing her arm.

Frankie turns to a fresh page, taking a *Home Away Inn* pen from her pocket. "Let's start with, *Hope you can meet us* . . . Where should we say?"

I think about how the best view of the Blythe Harbor fireworks is from the rocks at the tip of Spruce Point. It is *the* place to be, and people from all around come and line the beach to watch.

"Somewhere near here, but private. Oh, I know—*under the dock!*"

"Yes!" says Frankie. ". . . *on the Fourth of July* . . ."

". . . *at 9 o'clock!*" I finish.

Frankie repeats it all together, then writes it down.

Hope you can meet us
under the dock
on the 4th of July
at 9 o'clock.

As she dots the period, a loud clanking noise coming from the direction of Gruvlig's garage startles us. Frankie quickly blows out the candle. Huddled low, we strain to see into the dark night.

"What was that?" I notice I'm clutching Drake's hand.

"I think the ghost is trying to answer our questions!" says Drake.

"We need to investigate," says Frankie.

"Not me," says Sylvie. "I'm not going into moth world again. I'm staying here."

"Me too." Bailey climbs onto Sylvie's lap.

"That's fine," says Frankie. "Parker, Drake, let's go." I press my shoulder against hers, and Drake squishes right behind me, holding on to my shirt. As a clump, we move like a six-legged hunchback across the yard. Another metallic rattling sound halts our steps. When the noise stops, we inch forward again, past the hemlocks. Then we hear rustling paper.

"Who's there?" I ask, my voice clipped and high. I flick on the flashlight and aim it right at the sound.

"Oh!" says Drake, letting go of my shirt.

A big, fat raccoon has tipped over Mrs. Gruvlig's trash can and is enjoying the buffet of spilled garbage. He looks at us, bored, and keeps on eating.

I let out a relieved breath and sweep the flashlight back and forth, checking to see if he has any buddies with him.

We don't see any other animals, but we hear the noise of the garage door gliding open, and we scatter like bugs as weak light spills onto the driveway. The raccoon scampers into the shadows too. From my hiding spot, I see Mrs. Gruvlig, holding a broom.

"Who's there? Go away!" she shouts into the

darkness. Inside the front door, Napoleon is scratching frantically to get out, barking low and growling like he's in pain. Mrs. Gruvlig comes out onto the driveway and waves her broom in the area near the trash can, finding nothing.

It takes her a while to clean up the mess, and we stay hidden the whole time. Her long night-gown flows out around her as a breeze swirls in off the ocean. When she's done, she peers into the darkness, swaying and mumbling something. Finally she goes back inside, and the garage door rumbles shut.

Drake and Frankie and I come out of hiding and press close to her house, moving around the corner toward the site of the shell ring. It's still there, and Frankie carefully closes the two sides of the scallop shell around our note. That's when we hear it. A thin, quiet humming. Frankie grips my wrist, and I bite my lip to keep from giving us away.

A gust of wind bites through our thin summer pajamas. The rush of air through the pines makes a whooshing sound, drowning out the hum. Drake pulls the edge of my T-shirt and points at one of the first-floor windows. Gruvlig is standing in front of her fireplace, arranging rocks on her mantel. One, two, three, four, five. Biggest to smallest.

"Look," I whisper to Frankie.

Gruvlig swivels as if I've shouted, and we duck down, stay low, and *run*.

Later, after we've talked into the night and the others are asleep, I turn on my flashlight to record tonight's moon. Unmistakably, a flicker of brightness from Gruvlig's glints at the same time. I quickly bury my light and peer at the house. In the moonglow, I see feathery, misty ocean fog being pulled toward Gruvlig's cottage. Then with a whoosh in the opposite direction, the mist vaporizes. I keep staring, seeing nothing else unusual, until my eyes close on their own.

The sun burns bright and hot the next morning, baking us awake. We're rolling up our sleeping bags and Mrs. Wilkins has just come out onto the porch with bagels when I hear Mom's two-fingered whistle. Bailey and I snap to attention; we know that sound. It's not good.

"Kids!" Mom calls. "Come here, please. All of you. Now."

Mom and Mrs. Gruvlig are standing in front of the inn. Mom's arms are crossed, but Gruvlig's are flailing and pointing in anger.

"Uh-oh," I say.

We walk over to them on stiff legs, Mrs. Wilkins right behind us.

"What's going on?" Deb asks, looking into Mrs. Gruvlig's red face.

"I've come to ask you to control your children and keep them off my property. My trash can was tampered with, and this morning I saw footprints near the side of my house!" She wraps a thick, black sweater around her body, even though it's warm and sunny this morning.

"Hold on," says Mrs. Wilkins.

"Let's stick to the facts," says Mom. "Kids, Mrs. Gruvlig had some problems with her trash last night. Do you know anything about it?"

"Maybe it was a raccoon," says Sylvie. "They get into our trash all the time out on the island."

"I'd bet my last piece of candy it was a raccoon," says Drake. Sylvie tugs the back of his shirt.

"That seems to make more sense than the kids being over there," says Mom.

"What about the footprints? *Children's* footprints!" Gruvlig insists, pointing to our feet. "And last night right after it got dark, Napoleon was barking so violently I thought he'd burst his vocal cords. Spruce Point used to be civilized. Now it's overrun by vandals!"

"Hang on a second," says Mom. "I'm sure there's a logical explanation."

Mrs. Wilkins looks at us kids. "None of you have been over by Mrs. Gruvlig's house?"

"I was not near her house last night!" Sylvie says.

"We never touched your trash can, Mrs. Gruvlig," I say. We're both careful to state only the truth.

Mrs. Gruvlig twists her mouth and squints at all of us. "You kids stay away from my property. Stay away! *Or else.*"

She whirls on her heel and stomps down the front porch steps, like Bailey when she's having a tantrum. We watch silently as she slithers back through the hemlocks and into her yard. Mrs. Gruvlig's definitely someone capable of conjuring a major curse.

"Oh my. She's an interesting bird," says Mrs. Wilkins.

"I think she's sad," says Frankie, "and she doesn't know what to do about it."

"You're a smart young woman," Mom says, putting her arm around Frankie.

"And you both believe us, right?" Frankie asks. "We didn't mess with her trash."

"Well, I believe none of you would ever do

anything intentionally mean," says Mrs. Wilkins.

"And I'd like to believe you're all following our rules to stay away from her property," adds Mom. "Listen, let's agree to give Mrs. Gruvlig some space, okay? We've got our own problems; we don't need to borrow hers."

I nod, a tickle squirming in my belly. We need to be more careful. I can't give Mom and Dad anything else to worry about.

Chapter Sixteen

STORM WARNING

T HE HEAT AND humidity continue to climb, until it seems like every soggy spot on the point has been wrung out like a sponge into the air around us. By midafternoon, we're begging to go swimming.

"Okay, a quick dip before Uncle Paul runs you two back home," Mom says, pointing to the cousins. Drake frowns.

"What? Your mom misses you and wants to love on you!"

"That's what I'm afraid of!" Drake covers his face with his hands.

The day may be hot, but the water is still freezing cold. We all crash in off the shore together. I dunk under, and when I come back up, I have to scream to get the air moving in my lungs again. I kick my arms and legs so they don't turn into icicles. Bailey steps in up to her waist, then shrieks and retreats to the dock, where she sits hugging her knees.

"Race you to the raft!" Drake shouts to the rest of us.

"Wait! False start," Frankie yells, but it doesn't really matter, because swim-team Frankie easily zooms past him and is lying on the deck of the raft, catching her breath, by the time any of us get there. I sprawl on my stomach next to her, looking through the slats at the shadowy water below.

Frankie sits up and waves to Bailey. "Come on out with us, Lee Lee!"

Bailey shakes her head.

"It's not that far!" I call to her. "Last year you said you'd do it this year!"

"I just don't wanna right now," Bailey yells, turning her back to us. "It's too cold!"

"Come on, Lee Lee! You can do it!" Drake claps his hands.

Bailey shakes her head again.

"At least *try*!" I shout.

"She's still little—leave her alone," says Sylvie.

We stay out there a while longer, judging each other's dives, and counting "three, two, one!" before jumping together. I teach Drake how to swim up under the raft and rock it, and the girls squeal when we almost knock them off.

A small part of me is glad my little sister doesn't want to try swimming to the raft, because sometimes it's nice to have a little space from Barnacle Bailey. I stand up and turn in a slow circle. The shoreline that rings the bay to the left and right of us is dotted with a few people taking pictures or putting kayaks in the water. The big hill off to our left is bright with summer color. I look across to the southern side of Fox Island and see a huge motorboat pulling an even bigger sailboat out of the bay into the open water.

"I love it here so much," says Frankie on one long exhale.

I nod. If I could choose to live anywhere in the world, it would be this place. And I don't want anything to mess that up.

I see Dad come down the beach steps and stop to kiss the top of Mom's head. Then he hops into the skiff and revs the engine to call us when the boat is ready. We dive off the raft and race back, running up the dock with loud slapping feet.

Frankie grabs Bailey's hand as we climb into the boat. "How come you didn't come out with us?" she asks.

"I didn't feel like it today," Bailey says. "Maybe next time."

I roll my eyes, but Sylvie puts her finger across her lips and shakes her head.

Once we're away, Dad presses the throttle and spins us around, giving us a little thrill before taking off over the reach toward Fox Island. We pass Mr. Candage, who is out on his boat checking traps. When we holler hello, he tips his captain's hat and yells, "Hold steady!"

Aunt Jenny waves as we pull up to their mooring, and Sylvie and Drake hop out.

"Thanks, Uncle Paul," says Sylvie. "See you guys next weekend!"

"Bye," says Drake. He motions with two fingers to his eyes and then the opposite shore, and Sylvie traces the air like she's writing. Frankie and I both nod.

"Thanks, Paul, and watch out for that," says Aunt Jenny, pointing at a bank of dark clouds rolling in fast.

On our return trip, for a moment, I can see all

of Spruce Point at once. The flag in front of the inn is whipping wildly, and the weathervane on the cupola is spinning. Above the view it looks like a piece of charcoal has been dragged across the sky.

"Hang on!" yells Dad, and he guns the engine. From this angle, we can also see the curved bowl of the cove where the causeway bridge connects. Rain starts suddenly, coming across the bay in a distinct line. We crash into the wall of water and are instantly soaked. Dad struggles to keep the skiff steady as waves lift and churn around us. Something along the shore catches my eye. Faint through the sheen of rain, but undeniable. Wavering greenish splotches, moving among the pointy rocks along the cove.

I move my grip from the edge of the boat to Frankie's leg and shout, "The cove! Look!" into her ear. She pushes strings of wet hair out of her face to see and then turns to me with wide eyes.

I'm about to yell for Dad to look too, but I'm

interrupted when a bolt of lightning flashes out of the low-lying clouds and crackles right over the inn. At the same moment, the green lights disappear.

My stomach lurches as a wave hits us broadside. I don't think I've ever seen a storm come on this strong, this fast. And we're right in the middle of it.

Chapter Seventeen

LOST AND FOUND

"PARKER—GRAB THE rope! Frankie— bumpers out!" Dad barks orders as he fights to dock the skiff without crashing. Ocean spray and rainwater have swamped the bottom of the boat, and our feet slosh as we scurry to help. Another flash of lightning crackles.

I jump onto the dock and pull the rope tight around the cleats.

"Good!" says Dad. "Now go-go-go! You two get to the house! I'll be right behind you."

What I really want to do is run over to the cove and investigate. But there's no way that's happening right now. Ducking against the lashing rain, I lead Frankie around the edge of the meadow so we're not out in the open. We burst through the back door of the inn, filling the entryway with dripping water and nervous laughter.

"Oh, thank goodness," says Mom, pulling us to her and getting her own clothes wet in the process. "Where's your father?" she asks me.

"Right behind us." I shake my head like a dog, water splattering in an arc around me.

"You two stay right here. I'll go get towels," Mom says.

"You saw it too, right? The green?" I whisper to Frankie as Mom goes upstairs to the linen closet.

"Yeah, what *was* that? A weird trick of the lightning, some kind of electrical current?" Frankie moves to look out a back window toward the shore.

"If it was a trick, it's the second time I've seen the same one," I say. My soaked clothes feel heavy and a chill spreads across my skin. Maybe I wasn't dreaming the night the green mist pulled me after all.

The storm rages late into the night, and the next morning I wake up groggy. It's going to take me a minute to get my brain going.

In the kitchen, Dad is helping Bailey scramble eggs. Mom is sitting at the counter, squinting at her laptop and tapping a fingernail against her front teeth. The rain has moved off to sea, and weak sunlight falls across the mess of recipes and papers spread out next to her.

I drop a piece of Mom's homemade cinnamon-raisin bread into the toaster and lean my face over it, letting the warmth of my favorite smell smack me head-on. When it pops up, I slather on a thick layer of honey butter and take a bite.

Before I can swallow, I hear what sounds like a woodpecker knocking on our back screen door.

"Mornin'!" says Frankie, letting herself in. She

comes over and pulls on my arm. "I need to borrow Parker," she says to my parents.

"Hang on, I'm eating," I say. But she grabs a napkin and picks up my toast with it and swishes back out the door.

"You can eat on the way!" she calls.

I shake my head but slip on my boots to follow.

Once we're outside, Frankie hands over my slice of toast.

"What's up?" I ask, scarfing it in three bites.

"What's *up*? We need to go investigate those lights!" Then she presses her lips together and nods at Mrs. Wilkins, who has pulled alongside us in her car and is rolling down the window.

"Be good, you two. I'm going over to the antique store in Belfast for an auction, and I'll be back by dinner."

Frankie nods.

"Oh, and by the sounds of it, your dad is having a good writing morning. So only disturb him if it's an emergency, okay?"

"Gotcha, have fun, and yup," says Frankie. "We're all good here."

Mrs. Wilkins blows kisses, then continues down the gravel driveway. As soon as her car is out of sight, Frankie turns to me, her face shining.

"Frankenparker!" She grabs my shoulders and shakes them. "Hip-hip, elbow-elbow, head-shoulders-knees-toes-pop!" we say in unison, acting out each step.

We thunder down the slick beach steps and run along the pebbly shore, headed for the cove. Once we get close, we slow down and step as far out toward the water as we can, trying to remember exactly where we saw the green flashes.

"It was definitely, like, right in this area," Frankie says, sweeping her arm in a wide circle.

I walk to the end, where the beach rocks meet the concrete of the causeway. The watermark from last night's high tide is at the very top of the wall.

"Let's search from here to where it turns," I

say, indicating the curve that takes us back to our part of the beach.

"They were up in the trees. Right?" Frankie pushes back some branches, and collected rainwater from the leaves showers down on us.

"I think so," I say, pulling up my hood. But now that we're here looking, I feel increasingly unsure that we even saw anything at all. We come across a slight incline that seems to have had a chunk of earth washed away from it, like a mudslide.

I'm glad I'm in my tall boots as we squish and poke around in the slick mud, flipping unearthed rocks and shells to the side as we follow the path to the top of the crest.

"Whoa," says Frankie, falling to her knees, not caring about the wet seeping through her pant legs. "Check it out!"

I squat next to her as she pries a small wooden box from the hillside. She wipes at it with a big leaf, which doesn't do much to clean it. A small hinge has nearly worn off, and the top flips open easily. Inside is a model of a ship's steering wheel, about the size of a yo-yo. The eight small handles are made of brass, tarnished to a dusky brown. In the middle under a lightly scratched dome of glass is a compass. Frankie pulls it out by a long thin loop of faded leather that's been tied to one of the spokes.

Our cheeks practically touching, we peer at the find. I turn the wheel and the needle jiggles. "Now, *this* is definitely something the ghost of a sailor might have."

Frankie flips it over and runs her finger along the faint lines etched into the back of the trinket. "Wish we could read what this says . . ."

Caw-caw-caw. Gruvlig's crow flaps past and perches on a branch overhead. *Caw-caw-caw*, he cackles again. Frankie grabs my arm, her fingers digging into my skin. We take off running.

We push through the woods on a path of our own making and come up onto the bluff at the back of our property near one of the smaller cottages. Dad's walking toward us, carrying a wooden ladder. I nudge Frankie. She slips the cord over her head and tucks the compass inside her shirt.

"Hey, double trouble."

"You can't mean us," says Frankie, circling her hands in a halo above her head.

"Need help?" I ask.

"Sure, thanks bud. Hold the ladder for me? During that bad rain yesterday I noticed this gutter was totally clogged. I need to clean it out before we get another storm." He climbs up and I duck as he pulls out clumps of wet leaves left over from last fall and drops them to the ground.

Frankie squints up at him. "Mr. Emerton, who all has lived here besides your family?" she asks, motioning to the inn and cottages. "Do you know?"

"Well, if you're talking about property ownership, before me and Sarah it was my parents—Parker's Nana and Granddad. And before that, his great-grandparents, and before them, his great-greats. Our house hasn't always been an inn, but it's always been owned by Emertons."

"And it always will be—right, Dad?" I ask. But his eyes stay focused on his work, and he only grunts in reply. I squeeze the sides of the ladder.

"And what about the cottages?" Frankie asks.

"They were built when I was a little boy as a way to expand the family's hotel business. That's why they need so much maintenance now. Ha ha!"

"Think there's any way to find out who all has rented the cottages over the years?" Frankie asks. "Like, how far back do you think there are records?"

Dad comes down the ladder, shifts it to the left, and climbs again. "Well, Parker's Nana was known for throwing away anything that wasn't nailed down or being used. So, I'd guess not far. But I do know the cottage you stay in, Frankie, was rented by the same family for years and years. Finally they ended up building their own house on the parcel of land right next door. And they've kept that in their family too." He points with his head at Mrs. Gruvlig's.

"Really . . . ?" I ask.

"Yup. Believe it or not, Mrs. Gruvlig's son, Pete, and I were best summer friends, like you two."

Frankie and I exchange a look.

Dad's eyes soften with remembering. "We got into all kinds of good trouble, me and Pete. And every single Saturday, Mrs. Gruvlig made these epic blueberry pancakes. Any kid around was welcome to come eat."

"You're kidding!" says Frankie. "She *fed* you?"

"And she let kids in her house?" I say. "I don't believe you." Dad laughs.

"Wait, how come Pete never visits now?" Frankie asks.

Dad stops his work and climbs down. He leans back against the ladder and lowers his head, twisting his baseball cap in his hands.

"Well, after we all finished high school, Pete joined the navy, like lots of kids around here. He really loved it. Sad thing is, several years later he and two other guys drowned in a training exercise. Right near here too, in the very ocean we grew up playing in."

"Oh no," whispers Frankie.

"Yeah, it was a real tragedy. He was Mrs. Gruvlig's only child. I tried to give her my condolences, but she never opened her door or talked to anyone that summer he died. And as you know, she kind of stayed that way—private and quiet. Such a shame."

This is huge. Mrs. Gruvlig had a son! She was a *mom*. I try to picture her hugging and loving on a kid the way Mom does me. I can't do it. All I see is a witch, and darkness, and now sadness.

Dad finishes with the gutter, and we split up as he heads to the shed and Frankie and I keep going toward her cottage.

As we walk along the edge of the garden, something catches Frankie's eye and she stops short. I thud into her like a bumper car.

"What?" I say.

She points. "That was not here before." In the middle of the path between us and the garden fence is a stack of rocks, biggest to smallest.

"Another cairn!" I bend to get a closer look.

I pick up the top rock and squeeze it, rubbing the smooth piece of quartz with my thumb. Then I pause and turn to look at the inn, the cottages, and Mrs. Gruvlig's house. I slip the stone into my pocket. Whether it's good or bad, we are definitely not alone here this summer.

Chapter Eighteen

AN INVITATION

A FEW WEEKS later, Bailey and I sit at the kitchen counter, digging into our second helpings of Dad's banana pancakes while he pours batter for another round onto the sizzling skillet.

Mom looks up from the table, where she's making marks on three different lists she has going.

"You kids finish up and be ready to help unload when Aunt Jenny and the cousins pull in. She's bringing a bunch of extra stuff for this Jubilee Picnic that Dad and I've been planning."

Dad twists around from the stove and pushes an open page of the *Harbor Herald* toward me, tapping a quarter-page ad with a bold square around it.

"Turned out good, don't you think? Mom put it on the website, too."

FIRST ANNUAL JUBILEE PICNIC
at the Home Away Inn.
Celebrate the 4th with
independence from your kitchen!
• Land & Sea Cookout
• Traditional Games & More
• Steps away from the tip of
Spruce Point and the best
views of the fireworks
3:00 p.m.–The Finale
Tickets $10 / $50 family maximum
~~Come for the food,
stay for the view~~

Mom holds her coffee mug out for a refill, and when Dad takes it, I notice they're passing a frown back and forth too.

"So, what's the deal with this big picnic, anyway?" I ask. "We've never done it before."

They both stiffen and then paste on smiles.

"Well, this is the first time we haven't had a full house on the Fourth of July. So, since we have less work at the inn, I have the energy to organize it," says Mom.

"It'll be fun," says Dad. "And we'll make a little bit of money, too." He hands Mom her full cup, then goes back to the pancakes, mumbling under his breath when he flips them and sees how dark they've gotten.

A determined jolt zips through my body. I've been so busy trying to figure out what's going on at Mrs. Gruvlig's house that I haven't given the other parts of Operation Inn Keepers as much attention as I should have lately.

"I'm gonna go check on my pumpkins," I say,

sliding off my stool and out the back door.

In the garden, I peer down at the teeny-tiny sprouts in my pumpkin patch. I'm happy they've started, but it's hard to imagine these little things getting to prizewinning size in time for the fair.

Then something I didn't notice before catches my eye. Against the fence there's a bag of GroBest fertilizer that says, *Good, better, BEST! Your best fruits and vegetables—guaranteed.* Of course! Mom always puts fertilizer in the soil when she's starting up the garden.

I tip the bag over my sprouts, covering the area so you can barely see any dirt. I can't believe I didn't think of this before. I'm sure it won't be long now before my plants take off.

I'm finishing up when I hear the chugging rumble of *Adah Ruth*'s motor washing in on the breeze from the ocean. I run to the dock and see Sylvie and Drake on the bow, holding small American flags on sticks in the wind. Bailey comes along as they pull up, and she helps tie on the boat.

"Happy Fourth!" says Aunt Jenny, smiling at us and kissing Bailey's Betsy Ross bonnet.

"It's the third," says Bailey.

"You're right, but we're here to celebrate, so I say the party starts right now! Well, after you help me unload."

We take box after box of seafood into the large cooler in the kitchen. When the boat is empty, and the parents are inside, Frankie pops out of the front door of her cottage, claps her hands, and yells, "KCM!"

"KCM!" squeals Bailey. She and Drake jump up and down. "KCM! KCM!"

Instead of heading into the woods, Frankie takes off toward the water. We follow her down the steps to the beach and then under the dock, where we plop onto the cool sand. Drake opens a pack of M&M's and pours a few into each of our hands before tipping the rest into his mouth.

"We couldn't wait for you to get back," Frankie says to Drake and Sylvie. "I have called this Kids' Confidential Meeting because Parker and I have some amazing news to tell you three."

I bite my bottom lip and sit up on my knees.

"Is it that unicorns are real?" Bailey leans forward with fingers crossed.

"Shhh!" I say.

"Is it that we will be meeting a ghost? Right in this spot? Tomorrow night?" Drake pats the ground with each question.

"I hope that's true," says Frankie. "I hope it saw our note."

"This is something different, though," I say. "Frankie and I both saw some weird green lights flashing in the woods when we were coming home during that storm the night we took you guys back to the island."

"Lights?" asks Sylvie, head tilted.

"Yeah, and it's not the first time I've seen something like that. But this time Frankie saw it too."

"The next day we went to investigate the area. We didn't see the flashes again, but we did find *this*." She pulls the leather strap from around her neck over her head, and we all pass around the ship's wheel.

"Cool," says Drake, running his finger over the faint letters.

We hear footsteps above us, and Sylvie shushes us.

Through the slats, Aunt Jenny and Mom walk to the end of the dock with their late-morning coffee mugs. We stay still, and overhearing their conversation gives me a chill that has nothing to do with being down here in the shadows.

"Did you hear the causeway nearly flooded over again the other night?" Mom asks Aunt Jenny.

"Yeah, a lot of boaters were squawking about it on their radios the next morning," Aunt Jenny says. "People are really worried, Sarah, yours truly included. Climate change and sea level rise questions are all over my online boating forums. And apparently, some team from the state is coming to do a safety study of that overpass. But identifying a problem and finding the funding to fix it are two very different things."

"If they close that causeway, we might as well pack up," says Mom. "We'll basically be cut off from our main income source—tourists. The only other way to get here is to practically circumnavigate the whole dang state."

"You can't get there from here," Aunt Jenny jokes in a thick Maine accent.

"And you can't run an inn without guests!" Mom's voice is tight.

"Maybe when the water gets too warm and all the lobsters leave, I can start a ferry business for ya," says Aunt Jenny. But neither of them laugh.

The sudden clanging of our back-porch bell startles us, and we scatter out from under the dock, pretending we've been searching for treasures. I look up to see Dad motioning with one hand, the phone pressed to his ear with the other.

"Coming!" Mom shouts.

"Hey, kids, let's all head in and help start getting ready for tomorrow," Aunt Jenny calls to us.

As we cross the meadow, Dad hangs up and runs to give Mom a big hug.

"What's up?" asks Aunt Jenny.

"Hope that caffeine's kicked in," he says. "The whole town has been calling to say they're coming to the cookout!"

After that, there's no more time for ghost patrol or KCMs or anything else fun. We're all put to work, even Frankie, getting ready for tomorrow. We shuck corn, drag out the long folding tables, and help Dad put up some big white tents. When Mom comes back from the store, we're sent to unload the paper supplies and decorations.

All afternoon, deliveries arrive from everywhere on the peninsula. Mr. Bianco's meat truck is full of chicken, sausage, and hot dogs. The guy from Clover Hill Farm comes with all kinds of wildflowers, which Aunt Jenny arranges into mason jars to put on the tables. Mr. Wilkins turns up some jazz music coming from his porch, and it feels like the party is already starting.

I just hope our first annual Jubilee Picnic is not going to be our last.

Chapter Nineteen

INDEPENDENCE DAY

B Y EIGHT O'CLOCK the next morning, the temperature is already up to eighty degrees.

Mom has invited the Wilkinses over for breakfast as a thank-you for them being so kind about the fact that their quiet vacation spot will be overrun by the picnic today. She's laid out a small table on the front porch with muffins, fruit, juice, and coffee.

"It was weird to wake up without any guests at the inn this morning," says Dad. "First quiet

Fourth . . . ever? Thank goodness for you cottagers."

"Ha. We're the thankful ones," says Mr. Wilkins.

"Drink lots of fluids today, everybody," says Mom, refilling my juice glass. "It's gonna be a hot one." She finishes her coffee, then stands and claps her hands together. "Time to get to it, Team Emerton!"

"I'm gonna check my pumpkins real quick," I say. "Be right back."

"I'll come with you," says Frankie.

"Perfect—I was going to send you to grab me some dill for the potato salad," says Mom. "The rest of you kids go help Dad with the parking cones. T minus four hours till cookout!" She heads inside, whistling.

Over at the garden, everything looks neat and tidy, and I'm surprised because we haven't even been asked to help with weeding lately. I'm also psyched to see several flowers blooming on all four of my pumpkin plants. The vines and big leaves are starting to spread out over the patch too. I figure the fertilizer must be working, so I sprinkle some more from the bag right onto each stem. I wonder which of the flowers will actually turn into pumpkins.

"I'm supposed to choose one flower per plant to keep, and break off the rest," I tell Frankie.

"What? How come?"

"Mr. Melzen told me to. I guess so it can have all the nutrients to itself. That's what'll help it get monster big."

"How do you know which one to pick?"

Good question. Before I lose my nerve, I reach out and pinch off all but a single bloom on each vine. It feels good to have completed this step, but I hope the blossoms that are left are ones that will keep growing. I *need* them to. Because I *need* that prize money. I don't want to end up like the poor flowers I'd just plucked. I want to be the one that gets to stay and grow.

By late afternoon, it feels like everyone from Blythe Harbor is out on Spruce Point having a good time. Except Mrs. Gruvlig. When I glance at her house, I see she's out on her porch as usual, rocking in her chair, a dark knit cap pulled down over her ears. Napoleon's barking, and Gruvlig scowls at the visitors as she reaches for crab claws and cracks them open, picking away the sharp shell fragments with deliberate, fast movements. When she sees me looking, she scoots her chair so she's facing directly out to the bay.

Dad has both of the big cookout grills going, and the smell of spicy sausages and barbecued chicken makes my stomach grumble. Mom comes out of the kitchen carrying a huge stock-pot of freshly steamed lobsters, which she pours onto a serving table covered with newspaper.

Sylvie and Frankie are taking money and handing people tickets at the front of the food line. I'm holding tongs and standing over the warming trays of hot, buttery corn on the cob.

Between the steam from the trays and the blazing heat of the late-day sun, I feel like I might pass out. People parade past me in a blur, and I place a piece of corn on each large paper plate that is held out to me.

Finally the line slows down. Mom tells me I can get a plate of food for myself. I join Frankie and her parents at one of the long tables.

"Everything is so delicious," says Mr. Wilkins. "I hope your parents do this again next year, Parker! It should be a new tradition!"

"Ugh, hopefully it won't be so humid next time," says Mrs. Wilkins, swatting a fly away from her food. Mr. Wilkins winks at me and Frankie.

Across the field, Aunt Jenny blows a whistle. "Calling all kids! Game time!" Frankie and I ditch our plates in the trash and run over. Aunt Jenny organizes us in pairs for a three-legged race. Drake and a boy named Clancy from his class pull way ahead of all of us and get the first blue ribbons of the day.

After that there are races where we have to crawl like a crab, or balance an egg on a spoon, or pop a balloon by sitting on it before the next person can go. Finally we're split into teams for tug-of-war. Aunt Jenny calls for the adults to join in, and Dad takes the anchor of one side. Mr. Wilkins grabs the other. I stick my tongue out at Bailey, who is across from me on Dad's side. It kills me when they win.

"Ha ha, we beat you, weaklings!" says Bailey, pointing at me.

"Well, at least I'm strong enough to swim to the raft!" I growl, rubbing the painful red line on the palm of my hand. Bailey pouts and storms into the house.

As the sun disappears over the tall spruces and the sky becomes dusky, family groups find each other and wander down to the beach to set up blankets on the tip of the point. Boats begin to gather in the bay too, bobbing in each other's wake, lights blinking.

Mom, Dad, and Aunt Jenny are all busy cleaning up, so we join the Wilkinses on their blanket.

"Only about an hour to go," whispers Frankie, looking at her glowing watch.

"Where's Bailey?" asks Sylvie.

"Probably with my parents," I say.

A group of people nearby have brought hand drums and are forming a circle. "Can we go over and listen to the music, Dad?" asks Frankie.

"Sure," he says. "We'll be here relaxing and enjoying the pre-fireworks light show." He points up at the stars that one by one are poking holes in the darkening night sky. Mrs. Wilkins squirts bug spray onto the back of her neck.

Sylvie, Drake, Frankie and I pick our way through the crowd to stand near the drummers for a little while.

"Let's go to the dock now," whispers Drake. "I want to be waiting there when AG arrives."

"I really wonder where Lee Lee is, though," says Sylvie. "Should we look for her?"

"I'm sure she'll meet us there." I'm not going to miss out on the most exciting thing to ever happen because I had to stop and look for my little sister.

"It's getting pretty dark," says Drake. "What time is it, Frankie?"

Frankie looks at her watch again and then holds it out to us.

"Guys, it's time to meet A. *Ghost*."

Chapter Twenty

RESCUE

WHEN THE FIRST fireworks are launched, we hear *ooohs* and *ahhh*s and clapping. I peek through the slats from underneath the dock to watch a thin slice of the show. Normally, I wouldn't miss the fireworks for anything. But tonight is not normal.

We're all on high alert, aware of each stretch of silence between the explosions. We stare into the blackness, waiting for the flashes of color to light up the area around us.

"Hello?" Frankie calls urgently into the shadows. The wind blows an answer—pops and crackles mixed with murmurs from people farther up the point.

"Anybody there?" calls Drake, twisting to search.

"Maybe it's not coming," whispers Sylvie. She moves right next to me, our shoulders touching.

"Shhh! We're probably scaring it away," I say.

"We come in peace," chants Frankie. "Show yourself."

The waves lap against the posts of the dock, a rhythmic knocking. Then we hear a louder flapping noise, like hands hitting the water.

"What was that?" asks Frankie.

"Maybe a loon?" says Sylvie.

But birds don't make the sound we hear next. It's a cry, and a sputter, and a big splash.

"Hang on!" says an unfamiliar voice. "I'm coming!"

"Someone's out there! Let's go," shouts Frankie,

scrambling out from under the dock and pulling herself up onto it. We all follow.

When the next burst of color lights up the sky, we see two small shapes in the water.

Then, darkness.

Flash: One shape moving closer to the other.

Darkness.

Flash: Arms reaching up, arms reaching out.

Darkness.

Flash: One shape pulling the other toward us.

Darkness.

Flash: Two shapes right below us, next to the dock.

"Grab her!" says someone.

"Parker, help me!" It's Bailey. I lie on my stomach and reach blindly toward the sound of her voice. The fireworks crescendo into their finale just in time for me to make a grab for Bailey and haul her onto the dock. Frankie reaches out to the other swimmer.

For a moment, we all sit breathless and

stunned. I'm holding on to Bailey, who is crying.

"Are you guys okay?" asks Drake. They're dripping and shivering, but they both nod.

"What were you doing in the water?!" I yell at Bailey, fear making it come out like a sharp bark.

"I made it to the raft," she says between gulps and sobs. "But then I couldn't make it back. Then she saved me." Bailey points, and we all stare at the other kid.

I say the first thing that comes to my mind. It's not *Thank you for saving my sister's life*, like it should be. It's "Wow. You're glowing." I've never seen skin so white.

"Oh. Yeah, I know," the girl says. "But I'm not a ghost, I promise."

"Wait, what?" says Frankie.

"*You're* the ghost?" asks Drake.

"Well, yeah, but like I said, not really . . . Um, hi."

"*You're* AG?" I ask. The girl nods.

"Oh my gosh, you're actually here!" says Frankie. "Hi!"

"Wait . . . wait," I say. "What happened? Why were the two of you in the water?"

"I was coming down to meet up with you guys when I heard someone splashing around. It seemed like a weird time to go swimming, and when I saw she was having trouble, I didn't think . . . I just jumped in." AG pulls her T-shirt away from her body and twists the edge to wring out some of the wetness.

"*Thank you*," says Sylvie, rubbing her hands fast up and down Bailey's back. I squeeze my arms a little tighter around my little sister.

"You're really okay, Lee Lee?" asks Frankie. Bailey nods, still sniffling.

"And you're all right too, um, AG?" asks Drake.

"A for Adalyn," she says. "And just to be a hundred percent clear, not a ghost."

"You're definitely more angel than ghost!" says Sylvie. "Thank goodness you saw Lee Lee!" She kneel-walks over and gives Adalyn a hug. "I'm Sylvie," she says after she lets go. "This is

Parker, Drake, and Frankie, and the kid you res-
cued is Bailey."

Adalyn nods and smiles at each of us. "I'm
sorry I couldn't come over and say hi before. My
grandma is very protective of me."

"Mrs. Gruvlig is your *grandma*?" I ask.

"Yup. I'm spending the summer with her. My
dad used to spend summers here too. But . . . anyway . . . it's a long story."

Her dad—Mrs. Gruvlig's son, who died in the
navy accident?

"You've been here all summer? How have we
not seen you?" asks Sylvie.

"Actually . . . ," says Adalyn.

Before she can say more, we see flashlights
bobbing along the beach and hear our names
being called. Then the dock sways under the
weight of heavy, angry footsteps. A beam of light
waves wildly over our huddled group.

"Adalyn? Adalyn! Is that you? Get over here
right now. I didn't know where you were! You

scared me!" Mrs. Gruvlig shines her flashlight into our faces, and I blink and look away. Adalyn gets up and walks over to her. "You're wet! What happened? What were you thinking? Oh, thank the stars and heavens," says Gruvlig, her voice suddenly soft, her words gentle with relief.

Then two other dots of light bounce onto the dock. Dad and Mr. Wilkins take in the scene.

"I'd like to know what *all* of you were thinking," says Dad. He's talking to everyone, but he's looking right at me.

Chapter Twenty-One

DANGEROUS WATER

BACK AT THE inn, Adalyn and Bailey are bundled into blankets and we're all lined up on the couch in the front room. Mom fusses over Bailey, and Mrs. Gruvlig stands behind Adalyn, rubbing one of our guest towels through her hair with short, sharp tugs.

"Sorry for the troubles," Gruvlig says. "Adalyn should know better." She leans forward and whispers, "What have I said about usin' the brains God gave ya?"

"Well, I'm sorry she disobeyed you," says Dad. "But we are very grateful she *was* there. I have no idea what you were thinking, Bailey. Do you understand how dangerous that was? How many times have we told you? You never, never, *never* go near the water alone!"

"But I knew the other kids would be at the dock soon," Bailey squeaks. I tap her knee with mine and shake my head.

"I'm sorry, can we back up a moment?" asks Mrs. Wilkins. "Adalyn, is it? It's nice to meet you, honey. Um, who are you?"

"Adalyn is my son's daughter," says Gruvlig. "She and her mom have been living in Florida since Pete . . ." She shakes her head and pinches her lips together. "Anyway, Florida is not a healthy place for Adalyn anymore, so I've been watching her while her mom looks into relocating."

"Wow, you're Pete's daughter?" Dad's voice is clogged with emotion. "He and I were good buddies growing up," he explains. "I'm sorry, I had no idea he'd had a child."

"Yup, that's me," says Adalyn quietly, shrugging her shoulders. "Actually, he died right before I was born. And now Grandma Lizzy's all I've got besides my mom."

Grandma Lizzy?!

"We're all sorry about your dad, sweetie," says Mom.

Mr. Wilkins shifts forward in his chair. "So, have you been here long, then, Adalyn? We haven't seen you around."

"Um, a few weeks, I guess?" says Adalyn. "I'm a bit of a night owl." She looks up at her grandma. Frankie and I start to snicker, but a sharp look from Dad quiets us.

Mrs. Gruvlig grips the back of the couch and clears her throat, like she's going to give a speech. Then she relaxes her hands and puts them on Adalyn's shoulders. "You can tell, if you'd like."

"The thing is, I'm allergic to the sun," says Adalyn. "Like, for real. It makes me sick." She rubs her arms and looks around at our confused faces.

"At first I was getting little weird rashes, even if I'd only been outside for a few minutes. After a while, things got worse, and I was, like, really sick. That's when the doctors figured it out."

"What?" asks Drake, leaning forward. I think he's still hoping for some kind of supernatural explanation for Adalyn's nighttime antics.

"*Xeroderma pigmentosum*," Adalyn says. "People usually call it *XP*. I call it a pain in the neck. Literally. Anytime sunlight touches my skin, I become a hot mess. My mom wanted me out of Florida as soon as possible. So she sent me up here. Of course, there's still sun, but I will say there is a lot less of it in Maine than Florida."

"Especially in June," Mrs. Wilkins says. "You're right about that."

"Adalyn needs to be very, very careful now. I decided it's safest for her to only be outside at night," says Mrs. Gruvlig. "But even then, she is not supposed to go out without me." She makes a pinching motion at Adalyn.

"Sorry," says Adalyn.

"So, how was it that you all ended up together on the dock tonight, without any grown-ups knowing where you were?" Mom asks, her voice rising as she clutches Bailey to her chest.

I'm trying to decide whether to break my oath and tell them about A. *Ghost* and our bucket notes and shell notes and KCMs when Frankie chimes in.

"We were looking for Bailey. That's all." Her nervous fingers pull at the leather cord around her neck.

"No other reason," I add.

Somehow Adalyn catches on. "And I thought the dock would be a good place to see the fireworks."

"And I wanted to prove to Parker that I was strong enough to get out to the floating raft," says Bailey. My stomach lurches like I might throw up. I grab her hand and squeeze an apology.

"I'm sorry I caused trouble," says Bailey. She turns to Adalyn. "Thank you for helping me." They share a small smile.

Dad rubs his chin and pulls on his eyebrows. Mom lets out a big sigh and moves to give Adalyn a hug.

"Again, it wasn't right for your granddaughter to disobey you," Mom says to Mrs. Gruvlig. "But I am so glad that this time, she did."

Aunt Jenny comes into the room with a tray of coffee and hot chocolate.

"We're not through talking about this," says Dad. "But for now, let's take a moment to be grateful you're all okay." He lifts his mug. "To our new friend, Adalyn! Welcome to Spruce Point!"

We all reach for mugs to join in the toast, but when Mrs. Wilkins tries to hand one to Mrs. Gruvlig, she shakes her head. Something's wrong. Gruvlig's shoulders scrunch up toward her ears, her jaw clenches, and the lines that form her perpetual frown pull even lower. She's staring at the miniature ship's wheel that Frankie is tap-tap-tapping with her fingernail.

"*Where did you find that?*" Her voice is a whispered hiss, but it's more shocked than angry.

"I . . . near the cove. In the woods." Frankie's voice is tiny but steady. "There was a box."

"That. Belongs. To. Me." Mrs. Gruvlig holds out her hand, palm up. It's shaking.

Mrs. Wilkins moves to step in front of Frankie. "Calm down, please."

"It's okay, Deb," says Frankie. She pulls the necklace over her head and puts the ship's wheel in Mrs. Gruvlig's hand. "I'm sorry, I would have returned it right away if I'd known it was yours. I just found it, I swear! Right, Parker?"

I nod like I'm a bobblehead.

Gruvlig closes her gnarled hand around our find and holds it to her heart. She gives Frankie a sharp nod.

"Funny how things get misplaced sometimes," says Mom into the crackling silence.

Mrs. Gruvlig pulls on Adalyn's arm, motioning for her to stand. "We have to be going. Sorry again for the trouble."

"Please, stay?" Mom asks.

"We can't," says Mrs. Gruvlig. "I can't."

Adalyn looks around at all of us, then sets down her cocoa before moving to stand next to her stern-faced grandmother.

"It was nice to meet all of you," she says. Her gaze is on the floor.

"Please come back anytime!" Mom pats Adalyn on the shoulder as she walks the pair to the door.

"Bye! See you soon?" calls Frankie.

Adalyn looks over her shoulder with a sad smile as Mrs. Gruvlig leads her back out into the dark night.

Chapter Twenty-Two

BE OUR GUESTS

THAT NIGHT, SOME major things started shifting on the peninsula, kind of like the way the tide pulls and pushes, making the whole ocean move in and out. One thing that was not so great was that the following week felt muted and quiet, because Bailey and I were put in a chore-filled lockdown. Plus, the cousins left to go visit their New Hampshire grandparents, something they did every July.

One good thing was that, in a way, my

prediction about meeting the ghost being a way to break the curse seemed to be coming true. At least our phone had been ringing more this week, and future reservations were starting to trickle in.

When it rings again this morning, Bailey and I race to answer it, mostly because we want a break from the task that Mom had assigned today—washing baseboards. Bailey gets there first.

"Home Away Inn, the high point of Spruce Point," says Bailey in her sweetest voice. I give her a thumbs-up. "One moment, please." She hands Dad the phone.

He flips open the guest register and starts taking down the person's information. "Yes, there are two spots left in the class, and would you prefer an inn room or a cottage?"

When he hangs up, he says, "Yes!" and dances over to Mom, pulling her into a spin. "Two people coming for your *Decadent Desserts* cooking class today want to spend the night, too!"

Mom drops the trash bag she was holding and

lets Dad lead her, tango-style, over to me.

"Our idea man," Mom says, leaning to kiss the top of my head.

"Mr. Entrepreneur," Dad agrees. A warm feeling spreads through me, like when I slip into pajamas straight out of the dryer.

"Hey, what about me?" asks Bailey. She tilts back the cowboy hat she's wearing and taps the plastic silver badge pinned to her T-shirt. "I'm a sheriff—I'm helpful too!"

"Yup, we sure are grateful to have the law in our posse too," says Mom.

"Grateful enough that Bailey and I are free to go do whatever we want for the rest of the day?"

"Nice try," says Dad.

"Back to the baseboards," says Mom.

So, things aren't perfect, but they are heading in the right direction.

Another good thing from the past week is that Frankie used the time, as she put it, *to harness her power of persistence.* She went right over to

Gruvlig's the day after the incident and knocked on her door, and Gruvlig shooed her away, saying Adalyn needed rest. But being Frankie, she did not give up. She went back every day, multiple times a day, until finally Gruvlig told Frankie to come back Thursday evening.

Which is *tomorrow*. And I still need to convince Mom and Dad to let me go with her.

After lunch, Frankie and I are on my back porch, where she's watching me as I scrub sand off a mountain of mussels with a short, stiff brush for this weekend's dinner.

"I still don't get why *I'm* being punished," I say for the gajillionth time. "I didn't do anything wrong!"

"Bailey never would have tried for the raft if you hadn't been so pushy about it," says Frankie, shrugging. "I'd do your time and keep your mouth shut. At least you've been able to go outside." It's true. Bailey hasn't been allowed to leave the house at all.

"You can be really annoying, Francis," I say. "You gonna help me with these?"

"Nope," she says, "I'm too annoying."

I stick my tongue out and keep scrubbing.

By three o'clock, a few sets of guests have already checked in. There's an older couple here from Michigan. The other arrival is two college age-looking guys, one with a small bag and a guitar, the other with only a backpack. When they got here, the backpack guy, Dev, said he was looking forward to the cooking class, and especially learning about the history of Mom's recipes.

"I was so excited when I stumbled onto your website. I've been looking for an authentic culinary experience," he said.

"Does that mean you're looking for *dessert*?" Bailey asked.

"It can," he said, crouching to touch the top of her sparkly wand. "If it's the real deal."

Mom sends me to the shed by the big cottage

to get out the fishing gear for John, the guitar guy, since he won't be part of the class. We haven't had the best luck fishing from our dock, but lots of guests like to try anyway. John follows me, stopping from time to time to snap pictures of what to me are ordinary things.

I get him out onto the dock and am setting up the bait and hooks when I see the *Adah Ruth* coming across the water. It's Aunt Jenny with her regular delivery.

John reaches for his camera as the boat pulls in. He takes tons of pictures. When Aunt Jenny cuts the engine, he asks what it's like to drive a real Maine lobster boat.

"A lot better'n driving a fake one, I guess," she says. She hands me a big container of scallops for tomorrow's dinner.

"Your cousins say hi," she tells me. "They're having a grand old time getting spoiled by my ex in-laws." She waves goodbye, and John keeps taking pictures until the boat is only a tiny speck heading around the tip of Fox Island.

"Thanks for setting up this fishing gear for me," says John, finally putting down his camera. "I've actually never fished before."

"Really? Wow." I show him how to put the bait on and how to cast out. It always surprises me what some fully grown people don't know how to do.

He takes the pole from me, then pauses and stares at the bay. "You've got a little paradise up here, kid. I hope you know that."

Believe me. I do.

When I get back to the inn, Mom is telling Bailey it's her job to wash the dishes during the cooking class.

"No fair!" she says, adjusting her tiara. "Princesses don't do dishes!"

"They do if they don't want to be turned into frogs," says Mom, waving Bailey's wand over her.

"Why doesn't Parker have to help?"

"He does." Mom hands me an apron. "But

I promise, I'll take you guys for a swim after. *A supervised swim*. We'll all need to cool off!"

Helping with the class is actually kind of fun, because the whole kitchen basically turns into a sugar factory as Mom guides three different stations of people to make their own special blueberry desserts. I can't wait for Saturday when we'll get to eat the crisp she made as an example.

But the kitchen also feels like it's two hundred degrees. And as soon as the desserts are done and the class is mostly cleaned up, Mom keeps her promise.

"Let's go for that pre-dinner swim. Get your suits on, and see if Frankie wants to come too," she says.

"Really?" I ask. Mom is softening. I feel my freedom returning.

I change quick and run to knock on the Wilkinses' cottage door. Through the screen I see Frankie, wilted from heat and boredom, sur-rounded by chitchatting adults. Her parents have friends up for the weekend. She sees my swim trunks and towel.

"Yes!" she says before I even open my mouth. Then to her parents, she says, "Please?"

They agree, and she's changed and ready so fast I wonder if she was already wearing her suit under that dress Deb had made her put on.

John and Dev are already down by the water when we get there, tossing a Frisbee back and forth. Mom spreads out a big blanket near them on the pebbly sand, and Bailey flops down on it. Frankie and I drop the cooler of water that Mom asked me to bring, and the guys come over when she offers them a drink.

"Thanks," says John, perching on a nearby rock. "You kids want to use our Frisbee for a bit?"

"It's too hot to move," complains Bailey.

"Hot? This?" asks Dev. "Try spending a sum-mer in India!"

"Oh, seriously. You can't breathe," says John. "It's awful."

"What were you doing there?" asks Mom, opening a container of watermelon.

"We were there so I could learn more about regional differences in Indian food," says Dev. "My grandma taught me a few things growing up, but she didn't visit that often."

"Dev's an amazing cook," says John.

"Then how come you signed up for my mom's cooking class?" Bailey asks.

"Because a good cook never stops learning," says Dev.

"I'd love for you to teach me some things too, while you're here," says Mom. "I've never tried making Indian food at home."

"Sure!" says Dev. "That would be fun for me."

Frankie spits a watermelon seed from her last bite at me and says, "Let's go in!"

I make a big show of staying in the shallow water and playing with Bailey, calling for Mom to "watch me" every so often so she can see what a perfect big brother I am. Finally, she calls me over to her.

"Parker, you're exhausting me with your *good behavior*. I miss my real son!"

"Does that mean . . . ?"

"Yes. You can go see Adalyn with Frankie tomorrow. Just knock off the weird alien-son thing."

I make zombie arms and stagger toward her, grabbing her in a grateful hug.

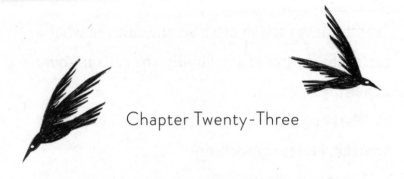

Chapter Twenty-Three

ENEMY TERRITORY

AFTER DINNER THE next day, following a strict lecture from Mom and Dad about staying off the beach, I go straight to Frankie's. When she joins me on the porch, I gesture over at Gruvlig's dark, buttoned-up house. "So we're supposed to just go over there now, like normal? Knock on the door?"

"Yes!" says Frankie, tugging on my arm. "C'mon!"

I hesitate, then decide I can't let her go in

alone. I amble over at half her speed and hang back at the bottom of the steps as Frankie raps on Mrs. Gruvlig's solid front door without hesitation. Napoleon barks, and I can't help thinking about how Hansel would have been a lot better off if he never went into that cottage in the first place.

"Get up here," says Frankie, pointing to the spot next to her. "She's not gonna bite."

"Which one?" I mumble as Napoleon's growls turn to excited yips. I climb the two front porch steps in slow motion.

"You're gonna be chill—right, Parker?" says Frankie.

"Of course!" I say.

"Don't ask about the XP thing. We're not gonna make it a big deal. She's a regular kid, got it?"

Living in a house with a witch, yeah, got it. "I'm cool. Don't worry."

The door creaks open, and Mrs. Gruvlig's voice comes from behind it. "Well, come in, then. Hurry up!"

We bunch into a small rectangular area created by heavy blankets hanging from the ceiling. Mrs. Gruvlig is holding Napoleon by the collar, hissing "*Quit that.*" Once the door is closed, she lifts the edge of one of the blankets and motions us through.

I blink a few times, my eyes adjusting to the dim light. Dark curtains and rugs cover all the windows, and the walls are blank. The air is still and smells like burnt toast. The one lamp in the living room shines a cool glow on the black, white, and gray furniture. It makes the whole place look like those beginning scenes in *The Wizard of Oz*.

"Hi, Mrs. Gruvlig," says Frankie, putting her hand out for Napoleon to sniff. "Is this a good time?"

"Yes! It's perfect!" calls Adalyn from above. "Come on up!"

With a sharp nod, Mrs. Gruvlig motions us toward the steps.

Walking into Adalyn's room is like stepping back in time. Faded images of ships' wheels on peeling wallpaper surround us. Model airplanes hang next to the dim overhead light, making weak shadows on the thin carpet. On a bookshelf there's a detailed model of a clipper ship, books about sailing, and several coils of rope tied into various knots. A small bed is pushed along the far wall, a gray cover tucked in sharply at the corners.

The only splashes of color come from some drawings taped to the wall and a collection of postcards safety-pinned to the heavy blinds that cover the window. Most have pictures of palm trees or white sandy beaches and deep blue water; one is a big cartoon orange with a speech bubble that says *Greetings from Florida!*

Adalyn pushes the door shut, then stands up against it. There's an awkward silence, and I stare at the ceiling fixture to avoid eye contact.

"So, this kind of light's okay for you?" I ask,

pointing. "You don't have to live in, like, complete darkness?"

"Parker!" says Frankie. "Please excuse him, Adalyn. It's apparently his first day on our planet." She turns to me with her fiercest *Zip it* face.

"I'm sorry!" I say. I can't help it. It's the only thought going on in my brain. "I meant . . ."

"No, it's okay," says Adalyn. "I know most people haven't heard of my condition. I get the curiosity. You two, honestly, are the first people I'm talking about it with besides my mom, my grandma, and the doctors. I'm still figuring stuff out. And I know it's good for me to be out of Florida, but Grandma Lizzy is like the sun police. I was so happy when you sent me that first note."

Frankie and I share a look.

"Yeah, about that," Frankie says, grimacing. "We're *so* sorry we thought you were a ghost! But things haven't been going great around here, and we got a little obsessed with this curse idea, and a ghost seemed to fit right into the story. . . ."

"Totally our bad," I say. "We did *not* mean to offend you."

Adalyn starts laughing. "I can't believe you thought that a ghost would be over there helping your poor scraggly pumpkin plants and making sure your clam bucket and shovel didn't get washed out with the tide when your little sis left them on the beach."

"That was *you!*" I exclaim. "I knew something was going on in the garden—we've never had so few weeds." I clasp my hands together. "*Thank you!*"

"Oh, and I can't tell you how many times I kept raccoons out of everybody's trash," Adalyn says. "Except for that one night—which was hilarious to watch, by the way."

"So all those times we were trying to figure out these odd events, it was basically you being helpful! Talk about opposite of a curse!" says Frankie.

Adalyn does a quick curtsy. "Ha, thanks. And

speaking of *curse*—I've been dying to ask you. What's up with this curse thing you guys keep talking about?"

"Well . . . ," I say.

Frankie puts her hand on my arm and stops me.

"Wait. First, we need to make you an official part of something important."

After a little practice, Adalyn raises her hand and speaks.

"*I, Adalyn Gruvlig, understand that Kids' Confidential Meetings are for kids only. I will resist growing up with every fiber of my being. This I solemnly swear.*"

"So, now you're one of us," says Frankie, plopping onto the bed. "And I declare this KCM open for business."

I stay standing, checking out the amazing drawings of Napoleon taped to the walls.

"Did you do these?" I ask. "They're amazing!"

"Yeah. I've had a *lot* of free time to practice." Adalyn sits on her bed with Frankie. "I've been drawing all kinds of things that I can see out my window." Her face gets serious. "And there's something specific I've been wanting to ask you about. Something very unusual."

Chapter Twenty-Four

IF NOT YOU, THEN WHO?

ADALYN LEANS OVER to grab a big spiral-bound sketchpad from under the bed and begins to leaf through the pages.

Frankie and I look on, and it's like seeing a scrapbook of our summer. There are detailed drawings of the inn, the bay at low tide, five kids running across the field to the woods, Napoleon in the yard, a clam bucket, the cottages, Frankie's dad on the front porch, Bailey in her Peter Pan costume. Everything.

"You've been watching us this whole time?" I ask.

"Well, yeah. I know that seems creepy. But there was nothing else to do, so I decided to keep a journal of sketches. I've been doing *a lot* of drawing this summer," says Adalyn.

She stands and lifts the edge of one of the postcards on the curtain. Beneath it is a thin cut that she pokes her finger into to show us how it opens. She squints her eyes and lifts one shoulder. "Um, sorry?"

"That's genius," says Frankie, getting up to have a look through the hole.

"It got to where I knew when anyone around here would be coming or going," says Adalyn. "And you people go to sleep soooo early in Maine! It got easier and easier to get out and do whatever I wanted once everyone else was in for the night."

She flips to the back of the sketchpad and continues. "But there were a few things I could never quite figure out. Like these." On the next page are several pictures of cairns.

"Wait," I say. "You didn't build those?"

She shakes her head.

"But you did do the shell rings, right?" Frankie asks. "We assumed the cairns were something like that."

"I love those little yellow periwinkle shells," says Adalyn. "I hadn't seen those in Florida. But those rock towers—that wasn't me. I actually thought you guys were building those. So that's one of the things I wanted to ask you about. And the other is these."

She turns the page. It shows a collection of greenish-yellow floating shapes. "What in the heck have you guys been doing that made such bright flashes?"

We all get quiet and search each other's faces for a moment. No smiling eyes. No one's kidding.

The warm air of her closed room feels suddenly chilly.

"That wasn't us either," whispers Frankie. She looks toward me.

"We've seen lights like that. Flashes and stuff," I say. "I've seen them a few times."

"What's it from?" asks Adalyn.

I rub my hands over my tingling goose bumps. "Well, I used to think I knew what it was, sort of. It has to do with the curse. But I'm afraid you won't like my theory."

"Why?" asks Adalyn. "Please, I'm so curious."

Frankie shakes her head at me, but I go ahead and say it.

"This is gonna sound wild. And maybe not so nice. But at one point I thought your grandma was the one controlling them. And that she was trying to make things bad for our business so we would leave and she'd have Spruce Point to herself."

Adalyn falls back on her bed and lets out a full belly laugh. Frankie picks up a pillow and hides her face.

"I'm . . . sorry . . . ," wheezes Adalyn between giggles. "That's . . . hilarious . . ."

She sits up and puts her hand on my shoulder. "Parker. My Grandma Lizzy is cranky and over-protective, but I promise you she's not into any-thing, like, occult or supernatural. She drinks tea and picks crabs all day and takes a nap every afternoon. She's boring!"

"Listen," I say with a shrug. "All I know is what I've seen. It's usually so dark over here, and that's why it was so noticeable when I started seeing flashes of light around the window edges. And because I've been tracking them, I know for a fact it always rains the next day. And the rain has been a disaster for everything around here this summer."

Adalyn fights breakthrough giggles and calms her breathing. "I don't know about flashes from inside this house and I'm positive it wasn't me or my grandma controlling anything. But that doesn't mean I don't believe you that bad things have been happening. And I agree those green lights are for real. They've been showing up on and off since I got here. So, please tell me everything you know. From the beginning."

Frankie and I take turns fulling in the gaps. All the way from the wreck of the *Westward* and the original curse, to the curselike things that have been happening on the point this summer. We even tell her about Operation Inn Keepers, and how we thought meeting her was going to be the key to completing the first item on the OInK list.

"Again, so sorry about that, Adalyn," says Frankie. "Obviously, no connection!"

Adalyn laughs. "Hey, I'm sorry to disappoint. Honestly, it would be cool to have that kind of power, wouldn't it? Think of the things you could change if you knew how to break curses!"

She sighs and rubs her arms. "But listen, count me in for doing anything I can to help the inn, okay? I know how hard it is to have to leave a place when you don't want to."

I chew my thumbnail and Adalyn tugs on her necklace, zipping the charm up and down the chain.

"The compass!" says Frankie, reaching over to touch it.

"Oh yeah, my grandma gave it to me," says Adalyn. "Guess what? It was my dad's!"

"I *never* would have kept it if I'd known that," says Frankie.

"I'm sure you wouldn't have! It's okay."

"What I mean is, I know what it's like. Having something physical to hold on to after a parent . . . you know. Is gone. I have my mom's favorite ring and it's irreplaceable." She pulls on her fourth finger. "Deb's my step-mom," she adds in explanation.

"Oh, I'm sorry," says Adalyn. "I didn't know we had that in common. It's not a fun club to be in."

I move to the window and look out through the hole.

"Don't take this the wrong way, Adalyn," says

Frankie, "but before we met you, I was kind of hoping you really were a ghost."

"I'm sorry I'm so alive and so normal," Adalyn says. Both girls laugh.

Frankie continues. "The thing is, it was pretty great thinking we might actually be communicating with someone who had died. Because . . . I wanted that to be true. I've always wished my mom could hear me when I talk to her. Everyone thinks I don't remember my mom that much since I was so little when she died. But I do, sort of. I mean, I think about her all the time, and I miss her!" Her voice trails off in a small squeak.

"I totally get that," says Adalyn. "I talk to my dad all the time too."

"Maybe your dad and your mom *can* hear you guys," I say, trying to be helpful. "No one knows for sure that dead people *can't* hear us, right?"

Ugh.

What am I doing? I'm probably making it worse. Why did I say the word *dead*?

"You think so?" Frankie sniffs.

"I think maybe it's like you said, where we're all too hung up on reality," I say. "There could be signs all around us, and we just don't know how to read or hear them. You're the one who said *anything is possible*. You still believe that, right?"

"Maybe you could, like, write a note to your mom?" suggests Adalyn. "I've done it before for my dad. Feels silly at first, but honestly, it was kind of nice."

Frankie nods and does a big snotty sniff. "I might. I have a lot of things to tell her."

"And what about your mom?" I ask Adalyn, pointing to the postcards. "Will you ever move back to Florida, or is it too sunny? Or will your mom move here?"

"Holy meatballs, Parker. Leave her alone!" Frankie's look says *Chill*.

"I don't know what's going to happen," says Adalyn, staring down at her lap. She rubs her hands up and down her thighs. "My mom has a pretty intense job. She's in charge of, like, a whole hospital in Tallahassee. She says it's hard to find the same kind of thing up here, and that I need to be patient. But I'd like to see her try being stuck alone inside with an old lady and a not-so-friendly dog *all summer!*" Her voice crackles, and I get that awful, gut-punch feeling that happens when you make someone almost cry.

"Well, not exactly alone anymore," I say, sitting down on the floor facing them.

"True! And good luck ever getting rid of us!" says Frankie, bumping her fist onto Adalyn's knee.

Mrs. Gruvlig's rough voice calls up the stairs that it's time for Adalyn's dinner.

"Darn," says Adalyn. She stands up, and we follow her as she makes a move toward the door. When her hand's on the doorknob, she turns around with a smile. "Wait! I have an idea!"

She takes one of the long coils of rope from the bookshelf and attaches it to the handle of a sturdy mug with a US Navy emblem on it. "I'll slip this out my window. If we have anything to tell each other, we can use this like you guys do your bucket."

"Great idea. If we put something in there, I'll call like this . . ." I do my signature mourning dove impression, *cooowah, cooo, coo, coo.*

"And I'm this," Frankie says. *"Wheet wheet wheet wheet."*

"Okay." Adalyn looks around. "I'll use this." She holds up an old boat whistle.

"Ooh, good," says Frankie. She writes out KCM's Morse code pattern for Adalyn. "Signal us anytime!"

Then we grab hands and teach Adalyn one more thing.

"Kids' Confidential Meeting—over. Grown-ups—never. Kids—forever."

Chapter Twenty-Five

INFESTATION

THE NEXT MORNING, Mom is up early and already busy in the kitchen when I get downstairs. She pauses long enough to put both hands on the side of my face and stare at me awhile. We do that sometimes—connect without words. Especially in the morning, when she knows I need a minute to get going. Right before I'm about to squirm, she kisses the top of my head and then spins away, reaching for one of her lists.

I watch her puttering around and am midway

through a bowl of granola when Mom opens the door to the pantry and yelps like she found a dead mouse in there.

"NO! No, no, no, no, no," she wails, waving her hands at the shelves.

"What's wrong?" I ask, rushing over. Bailey and Dad run in from the living room.

"Ugh, horrible pantry moths. Nasty devils!"

I look in to see a handful of small gray moths fluttering around where she keeps the flour and sugar.

"Gross," I say. "I'll get the fly swatter."

"Thanks, but there's a bigger problem with these pests. Once you see them, it's too late. Every single thing in here could be contaminated with their eggs." She looks like she might cry.

"We'll have to throw it all out," says Dad, shaking his head.

"Ew!" I glance over at my bowl of cereal, glad the container had come from a cupboard, not the pantry.

"Why? Why does something bad always happen when I'm busiest?" Mom asks. She grabs a black trash bag from under the sink and starts flicking boxes off the shelves into it.

Bad things always happen. Isn't that the definition of cursed?

Mom takes quick deep breaths. "Oh my gosh. Oh my gosh. There's so much to do! I have to clean to the studs and replenish our whole pantry supply, get rooms ready for the new guests, and prep a complete dinner!" She had decided to make weekend dinners at the inn for guests and people from town a regular thing. Like a restaurant, except instead of having menus, everyone eats whatever mom serves. She flutters her fingers against her legs. "Oh and I have to plan next week's cooking class too! Paul, I need you to—"

Dad puts his arm around her shoulder. "Hon. Hon. There's only one new set of guests coming tonight, and their room is already set up. Remember? And I'll go get a bunch of stuff from Broad

Arrow Farm to grill for tomorrow. I've been crav-
ing barbecue."

"And we'll go outside to stay out of your way,"
tries Bailey.

"Not quite," Dad says. "Lee Lee, you and Parker
can make up the beds and tidy the bathrooms
for the people who stayed last night. It's not like
you haven't been practicing for this moment all
week."

Bailey and I are finishing up when I hear Dad's
truck pull back in. I head out to help him unload,
and am surprised when I find him still sitting in
the driver's seat, his head resting on the steering
wheel.

"Dad? You okay?" I ask, climbing in next to
him.

"Oh, hey bud," he says, lifting his head and giving me a weak smile. "I wasn't expecting this turn
of events, that's all. Time is money, and I can't
afford to lose any of either. But now I won't have as

much time to work on that roof leak that's already taken me too long to repair. It's been a real pain, just like everything else about this place lately."

"Could you teach me how to do it? I can help."

He sighs and rubs a streak of dirt across his forehead. "Ah, look, this is not for you to worry about. But if you want to help, why don't you carry in these groceries and see if Mom needs any assistance with the whole pantry decontamination?"

I nod and hop out. I've never heard Dad talk like that. Right now, it seems like he wishes he'd never taken on the inn. That makes me wonder what else he regrets, and suddenly I feel kinda sick, like that time I ate too many hot dogs.

Back inside, I tap on the pantry door. Mom is sitting on the floor, wringing a rag above a bucket of bleach-smelling water.

"Hi there," she says, blowing her sticky bangs off her red face.

"Dad wanted me to check on you. He's working on the big cottage's roof."

"Oh, you sweetie," says Mom. "I'm doing all right. You kids okay?"

"We're fine, we finished the rooms. Hey, Mom, can I ask you something?"

"Mm-hmm," she says, leaning under the bottom shelf to wipe in the very back corners.

"Did you ever get something you thought you wanted, and then wish you hadn't gotten it after all?"

"Like what?" she asks.

"Like, maybe you ordered orange sherbet, because you thought it sounded really good. But once you tasted it, you wished you would have gotten fudge ripple instead. Except it's already too late."

"Huh? What are you talking about, hon?" she asks, straightening to look at me.

"Well, sometimes I wonder if you ever regret anything . . ."

"The only thing I regret right now is not planning out tomorrow's menu sooner. But I'll get it done. Eventually. After I go to the store and replenish everything I just had to throw away."

She pushes up to standing and dusts off her pants. "Stick around here in case the new guests arrive while I'm gone?"

I nod and she grabs her keys, muttering on her way out the back door about waste and inventory and moths.

The rest of the day and the next morning pass in a blur, with Bailey and I hopping from one chore to the next, helping Mom and Dad get everything ready for Mom's new "open dining room" Saturday night gig. The Wilkinses won't be here because they took their visitors over to Acadia for the day. But the third set of overnight guests arrive as I'm setting the tables, and soon after that, a handful of people from town show up too.

By the time everyone gathers in the dining room, I'm sweating from running back and forth with trays of food. We have a big buffet set up on the long table against the front wall: warm rolls, salad, corn on the cob, baked beans, and a towering platter of ribs and hamburgers that Dad grilled. The blueberry crisp from this week's class tempts me from a smaller table off to the side.

Dev is telling John how old the dessert recipe is, and other stuff that he learned in the class.

"Story is, the first thing a Mrs. Dolly Robertson did when her husband was put in charge of the post office in 1896 was to write home to her mom and ask for a recipe that would keep his eyes on his own dinner table."

Bailey is walking around offering people scallops wrapped in bacon. The lady from Michigan keeps saying how adorable she is. I think she just wants more of that bacon.

After supper, John goes to the porch and starts to play his guitar. Everyone else wanders out there too, and Dad sets up a few folding chairs. Some people lean against the railing. Mom has me carry tea and coffee to anyone who wants it. When I'm finally done, I stay to listen. John's really good, and he plays a long time because people keep asking for more. All his songs tell stories about being out to sea, or sailing, with lots of things about storms and fog and lighthouses.

Dad and I are on the porch swing, and I lean up against him. The new moon is out there somewhere, completely dark, and the cool night air dries off my sweat. I stare at the ceiling and pretend I'm on a ship, swaying back and forth in my hammock bunk. I like how I fit right into the bend of Dad's arm, like a puzzle piece.

> *Oh yes, I have a clipper ship,*
> *She's called the Henry Clay,*
> *Heave away, my Johnny, heave away.*
> *She sails today for Boston Bay,*
> *She sails away at break of day.*
> *And away, my Johnny boys,*
> *We're all bound to go*

Suddenly I sit bolt upright.

"You okay?" whispers Dad, rubbing his arm where my elbow dug in.

"Did you hear that?" I ask.

"What?"

"Other voices singing, besides John's."

"Huh. No." Dad turns his head to the side. "You still hear them?"

"No," I admit. "Not anymore." I listen for a long time, but don't hear anything else but John after that. Eventually, I relax again, and close my eyes. The rhythm of the swing and the strumming of the guitar lull me to sleep. I don't know how long I'm out, but at some point Dad jiggles my shoulder and walks me upstairs to my bedroom.

At my window, I use a combination of moonlight and flashlight to record tonight's moon phase. I see that the Wilkinses' car is still gone. I flick my light beyond their cottage, aiming it at Gruvlig's. A warm smile spreads when I see a tiny pinpoint of light winking back.

● ●● 232 ●● ●

I wake up the next morning hoping Frankie is back and can hang out today. I open my eyes and sit up, realizing I already have the answer.

She's standing in my doorway.

She springs onto the foot of my bed and bounces. "Get up get up get up get up!"

"Okay, geez, give a guy one sec . . ." The morning is gray and drizzly. I wouldn't mind staying under the covers a little longer.

Frankie flips on my bright overhead light, then pulls me to standing.

"Frankenparker!" she says into my face, shaking my shoulders.

I'm laughing as we *hip-hip, elbow-elbow, head-shoulders-knees-toes-pop.*

She's not done being pushy, though, and she keeps a grip on me as she sits me down on my desk chair. Then with a flourish, she pulls a book from where it was hidden behind her back in the waistband of her shorts.

"Look. What I. Found." With the tips of her fingers, she holds it out to me.

There is a silhouette of a black bird on the torn and faded cover. Underneath it is the title: *Paranormal America: Coastal Maine.*

"Whoa," I say, reaching for the thin volume. The binding is limp, and the pages are yellowed.

"I found it in this funky used bookstore we stopped in yesterday. It looked like a big old chicken barn, and the bottom half was all antiques. The grown-ups were taking forever so I went upstairs on my own and got lost in this like, maze of stacks, right? So, I'm in this back corner, and the very first book I pull out has Gruvlig's crow on the cover. Can you believe it? And look!"

She leans over my shoulder, opens to a page she has marked, and reads out loud. My eyes follow the words.

"*The coastal area known as Down East is well known for having spikes of paranormal activity, especially in the summer months. Some theorists* suggest reported happenings can be attributed to the ghosts of sailors lost at sea wandering the shores, looking for their homes."

"That's like the story Dad tells!" I whisper. "The crew of the *Westward*!"

For the rest of the morning, Frankie and I take turns reading out loud to each other. The book is full of stories about weird things people have reported seeing or experiencing. Lots of them are about objects moving without being touched. One of them is about a lady who kept seeing someone else's reflection in the mirror.

But then we get to a part that actually makes my hands shake a little, so that the booklet quivers and Frankie has to take it from me so she can finish reading to the end of the section. Her voice rises higher and higher as she does.

"*For some, these occurrences are unwelcome,*" she reads, "*but others have experimented with ways to strengthen the connection to and harness the power of the supernatural. These attempts include* the gathering and placement of rocks, wood, or other natural elements in ceremonial towers or rings. Water also plays a key role."

"Wow," I say. I'm picturing all the cairns.

"It's like you said before," says Frankie. "Not all the messages being sent this summer are written in words."

I stand up. "Someone's trying to tell us something, Frankie. And we need to figure out how to listen."

Frankie nods. "Let's go send a message to Adalyn. And the cousins will be back this week, right? We're going to need everyone's help."

At that moment, a clap of thunder crackles through the thick humid air, and the power to the whole point goes out.

Chapter Twenty-Six

OFF THE GRID

W E HEAD DOWNSTAIRS and find Mom already in "outage" mode, pulling candles and batteries from the chest of drawers near the fireplace.

"I had no idea it was supposed to storm today," she says, trying flashlights.

"Me either, but it's whippin'," says Dad. He has the front door open to assess the situation, and the smell of fresh morning rain makes itself at home in our living room. We can hear the floating buoys being tossed around.

Mom puts a flashlight with fresh batteries and a big pillar candle with a pack of matches onto a stack of blankets and towels and hands the whole pile to me.

"Take these over to the bay cottage for me, before this weather gets worse, would you?" she asks. "John and Dev are staying in the area a little longer, and they've decided to set up here."

"I'm glad they're not leaving yet," says Bailey from her perch by the fireplace where she's breaking up sticks for kindling. "They're nice."

"Remember to stay out of their way, though— okay, kids? They're here on vacation," says Dad.

"Not John," says Bailey. "He said he's working, searching for sailor songs."

"*Researching,*" Mom corrects. "He told me he's writing an article about sea shanties for *Coastal Traditions* magazine!"

Frankie takes half the pile from my arms. "I'll help you, Parker."

Mom drapes us with big ponchos she keeps in a front closet for visitors, and we dash through the blowing rain.

When we clomp up the deck stairs, Dev opens up the screen door and takes our bundles, urging us to come in. John is on the love seat in the bay window, playing guitar. He smiles at us and we stand in the foyer, dripping onto the tile floor and listening.

Away and to the westward
Is a place a man should go
Where the fishing's always easy
They've got no ice or snow

But I'll haul down the sail
Where the bays come together
Bide away the days
On the hills of Isle au Haut

Now the winters drive you crazy
And the fishing's hard and slow

You're a darned fool if you stay
But there's no better place to go

We clap when the song ends, and John nods his head in a bow.

"Hi, Mr. John," says Frankie.

"Mornin', kids," he says, lowering his guitar. "What's the word?"

"My mom said to bring these extra blankets and supplies to you," I say. "Sorry the power's out. It does that. Should be back on soon."

"Hey, thanks. We're so psyched to be staying longer," says Dev. "There's so much to see and do around here. And John found a music lending library that's perfect for what he's working on."

"Do any of your songs talk about the ghosts of sailors walking around looking for their homes?" Frankie asks.

"Not exactly, but a lot of them warn about getting lost at sea," John says. "Are you interested in stories like that?"

Frankie slips *Paranormal America: Coastal Maine* out of her waistband and holds it up, tapping the spine. "Definitely."

"Ooh, can I have a look?" asks John.

Frankie glances over at me and I nod. She hands him the book.

He whistles as he runs his fingers over the fraying cover. "What a treasure!" he says, peeking inside. "Wow. This is old!"

Dev has gone to put the blankets down and when he comes back, asks, "Do you two want some breakfast? I made plenty . . ."

"No thanks, Mr. Dev. We're good," says Frankie.

"Sorry," I add. "We should go. We're not supposed to be bothering you."

"You're not a bother. You're welcome to stop by anytime," says Dev.

"Yeah, I'd love to have a closer look at this book when you're done with it. May I?" asks John.

"Sure," says Frankie. "But we need to show it to the other kids first."

"No problem. Whenever. I think you might have just given me an interesting angle to write my article from!"

After we leave a note updating Adalyn about Frankie's find, we go back to the inn, where Mrs. Wilkins is waiting for Frankie in the front room. She's come over to tell her they'll be going up to the Bangor Mall and staying at a hotel until the power comes back.

"C'mon, Deb, we can survive a while without power!" Frankie plants her feet. "The Emertons aren't leaving!"

"That's because the *Emertons* come from strong, resilient people," says Mrs. Wilkins, smiling at Mom. "I, however, come from a people for whom indoor camping is not tolerable. And your father is nervous about keeping his laptop charged. Heaven help us if that man lost any of this morning's writing . . ."

"I have to admit, it does seem like a good

time to get away," says Dad, peering out at the blustery day.

As they walk down our porch steps huddled under an umbrella, I hear Mrs. Wilkins tell Frankie, "We'll set your father up at the coffee kiosk, and then we can shop till we drop!"

Frankie looks back at me, crossing her eyes. I give her two thumbs-up.

"Good luck!" I call.

I pull the front door closed and go to the window seat to watch the storm. Soon the rain starts coming at the side of the inn in big sheets, like a bucket of water is being thrown at us, over and over. The yard has started to crack into giant fingerlike streams of sandy mud. I watch the Wilkinses' car pull out and disappear down the lane.

"I told Jenny to hold deliveries until this calms down," Dad tells Mom. "No one should be out on the water in this mess. That okay with you?"

Mom nods. "I won't need the extra lobsters

until Wednesday's *Seafood Soups & Chowders* class, anyway."

She's moving around the living room, setting out candles of all different sizes and shapes for when it gets dark later. She freezes mid-motion. "Oh, Paul! My class! What if the power doesn't come back!"

Dad walks over and kneads her lifted shoulders with his thick fingers. "It's a quick summer storm, that's all. Power won't be out for long. And if it is, I'll get you a nice fire going in the main hearth, and you can switch the class name to *Off the Grid Chowders*. People from away will eat that up. Get it? Eat it up?"

Mom turns to give him a peck on the cheek. "Okay, I won't panic yet. But I think I'll get a head start on planning things, just in case."

I move to join Dad and Bailey at the kitchen table for a game of Go Fish, while Mom putters around us, clearing off the long center counter and setting up four more or less identical cooking stations. Each time she puts something down, she looks at it, sighs, and then rearranges how things are positioned.

"This next class will be a little more complicated than blueberry crisp. But it'll be fun, teaching again. Won't it be fun?" she asks.

I open my mouth to answer, but Dad takes over.

"You're going to be amazing, honey. There's nothing to worry about."

"I'm not worried!" says Mom, her head now buried in the pantry. She's moving cans around from one shelf to another.

A huge gust of wind makes us all stop and look outside.

"Well, *I'm* worried—about my pumpkins," I say. Plants have very predictable growing schedules, *if* you can control all the parameters, that is.

"Yeah, this is a lot of rain for a little newbie crop," says Dad, "but there's not much we can do. I sure hope that the seeds that were gonna take root already have."

We spend the rest of the day reading and prepping for a night without electricity. I lug jugs of water from the basement for every bathroom, and Dad lays a fire in the fireplace, adding to Bailey's kindling. Mom makes sure each bedroom has its own working flashlight.

Later that evening, when the gray light coming in the windows turns to black, Dad stokes the fire and Mom moves around the first floor, lighting the candles she's set out.

"Hmmm . . . popcorn for dinner?" asks Mom.

"Yes!" Bailey and I shout.

We pull cushions up around the fire, and Mom puts oil and kernels into a metal pot with a long handle. Bailey and I take turns shaking it over the flames.

"This was Granddad's popcorn popper," says Bailey.

"And you used to take it on camping trips with you growing up," I say to Dad.

"And you made me popcorn on our first date," says Mom.

"All true," says Dad. "That old thing has a lot of memories in it."

"Like this house does too," I say.

"The handle's loose," says Bailey, wiggling it.

Mom reaches over and tests the jiggle. "Hmm . . . might need a replacement soon. It would take some hunting around antique shops, but I'll bet we could find something similar."

"No!" I say. "It wouldn't be the same. We have to keep this exact one." I take it from Bailey and shake it harder over the fire.

"It's funny to hear you say that, Parker," says Mom. "You always tell me how much you like the microwave kind."

"Well, I don't anymore," I say. "I like things how they are. Right now."

Mom and Dad exchange a look. Then the kernels start popping, and I have to focus on keeping the pot moving so everything won't be ruined.

Chapter Twenty-Seven

SABOTAGE

O N WEDNESDAY, A thick fog replaces the rain. Our power came back on sometime in the night, and it's bright but quiet in the kitchen. Dad is moving around like a pajama-wearing ninja, trying not to disturb Mom's class setup. Bailey is under the table with a bunch of stuffed toys.

"Where's Mom?" I ask, sniffing for something better than the cold cereal that Dad just took from the cupboard.

"Slight problem. She got this big thing of

cream for today's class, but when she poured some into her coffee this morning, it curdled. So she had to go out for more. Then her car wouldn't start. Not a great morning so far."

"Ah, gotcha. Steer clear." Dad nods with a wink. I shovel in my cereal and avoid catching Bailey's attention as I head out the back door to check on my pumpkins.

The garden is a big, flooded mess. The potato mounds are squished flat, and there are puddles polka-dotting the whole area. The biggest divot even has a bird splashing in the dirt-swilled pond that's been created.

"Dad, look at this!" I yell. He's on his way to check on the garden too.

He clicks his tongue. "We definitely won't have to water anytime soon. Let's see what we can salvage."

What we need is a hot sunny day to help dry out the soil. But the fog is like a big wet blanket, holding all the moisture close to the ground. So,

I do what I can. First, I use a trowel to scoop water out of my planting bed, like I'm bailing the bottom of a boat. Then I mound up the soil around my plants as high as I can. That might help if we get hit with another storm like this last one.

My arms are streaked with dirt all the way up to my elbows, and my boots are covered in it too.

"I'm going down to rinse off."

"Good idea, Mud Monster," says Dad.

I leave a clumpy trail of footprints on the beach steps and across the rocky sand on my way to the ocean's edge. I plunge my hands into the freezing Atlantic and rub as fast as I can. My skin tingles, like I'm being jabbed by sharp needles. I stand and pull my arms inside my shirt, tucking my icy palms under my armpits. *Brrrr.*

Inside the thick cloud of fog, I pretend I'm completely alone, a new arrival on a deserted planet.

"Hello!" I call out to the bay. In the silence that follows, loneliness tugs on me like a wave being pulled out by the tide. Then I hear a scraping noise behind me. I turn but can't even see as far as the bottom tread of the beach stairs.

"Who's there?" I ask into the white mist.

Clunk, drag. My legs shake, the bare skin below my shorts crawling with that goose-bump feeling.

"HELLO?" I yell louder. This time there's an answer.

It's the familiar clanging of Aunt Jenny's boat, coming in slow. I run out to the end of the dock and yell, "Marco!"

"Polo!" Drake's voice calls back. A thin beam of light cuts toward me.

We Marco-Polo until the *Adah Ruth* whispers in alongside where I'm standing, and Drake throws me a rope.

"Hey, Parker, guess what?" Sylvie holds up a big duffel bag.

"We're off-island!" says Drake, popping a butterscotch into his mouth.

"For real?"

"Yup," says Aunt Jenny, handing me a crate. "They're saying the island might be without power for quite a while. I personally don't mind pioneer living, but—"

"We can't even flush the toilet!" interrupts Drake, pinching his nose.

"No toilet! No refrigerator! Reading by candlelight! It's like an episode of *Little House on the Island* out there," says Sylvie.

"There was a mutiny among the troops," says Aunt Jenny, flinging her bag onto the dock.

"Yeah, and Mom said we could stay with you guys if Aunt Sarah says it's okay, because since we got back from New Hampshire, we've been driving her batty begging her to come back here so we can be with you guys and our new friend the ghost!" Drake jumps onto the dock.

"She's not a ghost!" Sylvie corrects him. "But I agree, we couldn't wait to get back. We're dying to hear what's been going on. What did we miss?"

As Aunt Jenny secures the boat, I pull the kids to the side and finger-spell *K-C-M.*

"Tonight," I whisper. We have a lot to tell them.

Up at the house, Mom is sitting on a kitchen stool, chewing on her thumbnail and jiggling her foot. Her hair is up in a clip that has fallen off to one side.

"You look awful, Sarah. No offense," says Aunt Jenny, helping herself to a cup of coffee from the pot on the counter.

"Car battery was dead this morning, and then I had to go to two different stores to find enough fresh cream. The soup class and dinner tonight are the only additional business we've had this week, so things have to be perfect!"

Sylvie and I look at each other.

"At least the power's back on," I say. Mom nods.

"And your fresh seafood and fresh recruits have arrived," says Aunt Jenny. "We got this."

Bailey and I help the cousins carry their bags

upstairs to our bedrooms, and from the window I watch four unfamiliar cars pull into the parking area out front. The cooking class students are here. I study the license plates. Two Maine, one Massachusetts, one Connecticut. This is good. People from away might see the inn and like it better than where they're staying now, maybe even enough to change their plans mid-vacation.

Drake and Bailey stay upstairs, but Sylvie and I head down to help. The students are all quiet at first, nodding at each other and looking around the kitchen. Then Mom tells them a little about the Home Away Inn, and how the recipes are from the grandmother of these kids standing right here, so they can blame us if anything doesn't taste right. Everyone laughs and seems to relax.

When the actual cooking starts, Sylvie and I are busy grabbing ingredients, running stuff to the sink for Aunt Jenny to wash, and doing anything else Mom asks us to do. The time flies. A few hours later, we wave from the porch as the people get back into their cars, balancing containers of fresh soup. They're all smiling as they drive away.

While Mom and Aunt Jenny clean up, Sylvie and I call Drake and Bailey for a KCM in my room so I can fill them all in on what's been happening around here.

"Okay, listen. Quick summary before we meet up tonight. Adalyn's cool; Mrs. Gruvlig is cranky but not a witch; Frankie and I saw the weird green lights, which led us to finding buried treasure—a ship's wheel compass that apparently belonged to Adalyn's dad. Conclusion: We still think there's something odd going on around here, namely that some 'thing' is harnessing power and causing trouble for Spruce Point.

"Also, importantly for you, Miss Sylvie the Skeptic," I say, "I have some very special show-and-tell."

I pause for effect, then pull out *Paranormal America: Coastal Maine*.

"Cool! Where did you get that?" Drake asks.

"Frankie found it at an old used bookstore that's probably haunted, where else?"

I point out the section about the ghosts of sailors who were lost at sea and the part about rock towers being used to connect to supernatural energy before Sylvie snatches the book and shushes me so she can read more.

When we hear the crunch of car wheels on gravel, we all press against my bedroom window and cheer.

Frankie's back.

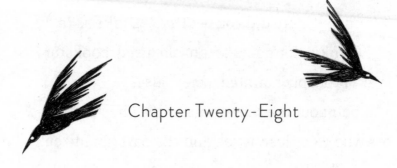

Chapter Twenty-Eight

ADALYN TIME

AFTER DINNER, WE pace around the front
yard. It's nearly impossible waiting for what
I think of as *Adalyn time* tonight. It's been a few
days since Frankie and I were over at her place,
and I can't wait for her to *really* meet the cousins,
and Bailey, and for them to get to know her. Now
our group will be complete.

I peer at the sky, willing the setting sun to
hurry up and make way for tonight's growing
waxing crescent, which looks like a thin slice of

a giant's thumbnail. As I mark it off in my journal, Adalyn's whistle sounds. We walk toward Gruvlig's and watch while Adalyn's grandma gives her like a five-minute lecture before finally releasing her.

"To the fort!" calls Drake, and our bobbing line of flashlights heads off into the woods.

The darkness closes in around us, reminding me of the time I came out here alone the night of the super blood moon. An owl sounds and a bullfrog answers. Mosquitoes close in.

"Look at that," says Frankie, waving her flashlight beam on the dozens of webby blobs hanging in the trees, making them glow. The way they drape off the branches and sway in the breeze reminds me of tissue-paper ghosts at Halloween.

"Gee, that's not creepy," I say.

"What are those things?" Bailey asks.

"It could be the brown-tail moth nests everyone's talking about this summer," says Sylvie. "So be really careful not to touch them."

"They can mess with your breathing," I say, nodding.

"Moths *are* known for being a symbol of death," says Adalyn, stepping closer.

"Okay, thank you for that. Very helpful." I rub my arms.

We stand still a moment, watching the nests sway and listening to the chittering and creaking sounds of the night forest.

"OooOOooo!" Drake jumps out in front of us holding his flashlight under his chin.

"Drake, no, stop!" says Bailey. She barnacles onto me, and this time I don't mind.

"Quit playing, guys, let's keep going." Frankie pushes on ahead, and the rest of us stick together in a close clump behind her.

When we get to the tree house, we crowd onto the platform and Frankie has us all recite the KCM oath. Then she motions for us to sit down and says, "Okay, open for business! We have an inn to save and a curse to break. Who's got what?

Parker—Operation Inn Keepers. Report."

I pull out our notebook and open to the *OInK* list I had taped in there.

OPERATION INN KEEPERS: OInK
1. Break curse
2. Advertise (poster) and get more guests
3. Cooking class—Mom
4. ?? Win pumpkin prize money

"Okay, so," I say. "The cooking class thing is working, but we are way low on overnight guests and we have two cottages still sitting empty. Anyone have anything else to report?"

Frankie nods and leans in to tap her finger on the last three items. "Well, we've got an ad up, and you guys can definitely help with the cooking class again. And the pumpkin patch looked pretty good last time I saw it."

"Right, so that's a maybe," I say. "But this

one . . ." I point to our first item and the word *curse*. "Every time something good happens, it feels like something bad comes right after. It's like we can't get ahead.

"And I'm glad you're not a ghost and all, Adalyn, but I feel like that puts us further away from figuring this out."

"You're right, Parker," Frankie says. "We know now that none of it actually has to do with Adalyn or her grandma." She smiles at our new friend. "But that doesn't mean there's no curse. So let's talk about that. What *do* we know?"

I tick off the list on my fingers: "Tons of rain, a flooded road, spoiled food, moth infestations— plural, miserable garden, power outage, not enough guests, stressed parents."

"My mom's been more worried lately too," says Sylvie. "Things are still slow."

Frankie crosses her arms. "It sure seems like there's some force hanging around, waiting to ruin things. But what does it want? How will we break the spell if we don't even know what we're dealing with?"

Adalyn spreads her hands and shrugs. "According to all of you, the only new things here this summer, besides me, are those mysterious flashes of light, and the cairns. I say we focus on them."

"I haven't seen any lights," says Bailey. "And I think the *carings* are pretty. Mrs. Rhoades says sharing is caring. We should build one too."

"No!" says Drake, crinkling open a lemon drop. "What if that book's right about them being used in ceremonies to gather supernatural energy? Those rock towers could be strengthening the curse! We should stay away from them."

"Um, too late?" says Sylvie. She'd moved to the back corner of the platform to stretch out her legs. Her flashlight beam shows us what she's talking about.

"Look!" says Adalyn.

It's another set of rocks. Biggest to smallest,

but laid flat and stretched out in a line like an arrow instead of stacked like a cairn.

Frankie lets out a long, low whistle. "Were any of you here earlier? Did one of you do that?"

We all shake our heads.

"It looks like the rocks are pointing that way," says Adalyn, tilting her head from where she's squatting on her haunches to get a close-up view. I follow her line of sight and look over the railing into the woods.

When a breeze flutters the leaves, we can see the inside lights on at the bay cottage in the distance.

"That's the cottage those two guys are staying in, right?"

"John and Dev," I say. "They're both super nice."

Adalyn nods. "So, not to sound like a creeper, but I can see that cottage from my window. I love it when that one guy comes out to the porch to play guitar. It's awesome how clearly I can hear him, especially when the wind is blowing my way.

Kind of like having my own personal concert."

"I like when he sings," says Bailey.

"Me too. And you know how he's always sing-ing those same kinds of songs about ships and the ocean?" asks Adalyn.

"Sea shanties. He's researching them," I add.

"So here's the thing. See, it occurs to me, the flashes of green always seem to happen on nights he's out there, singing those old sailor songs." She starts to hum the tune of one, and my stomach does a flutter kick.

"Well, that's a twist," says Frankie. "And John was super excited to borrow our *Paranormal America* book."

"Plus, the rains almost always come right around the same time the lights flash," I say, checking my chart.

Frankie starts to pace. "My dad would say that both things you guys are talking about could be *true, true, and unrelated*. Like, there might be songs followed by flashes of light, or flashes of light followed by rain, but it doesn't mean one thing causes the other. We'd need to find some evidence connecting the two."

"I never knew curse breaking could be so confusing," says Drake.

"You know," Adalyn taps the ship's wheel around her neck, "every Thursday evening since they got here, the guitar guy and his buddy leave at six thirty and come back a few hours later."

"Oh, the *Thursdays on the Lawn* thing at the library—they always talk about how much they love those concerts," I say.

"That's tomorrow!" Frankie says.

"It'll be too early for me to go out," Adalyn says. "But it might be a good time to do some investigating. You know, if you know of anyone interested in doing something like that."

We all grin and pull our circle closer. As we plot our next few actions and the night fog rolls in to cover the forest floor beneath us, the Spruce Point Ghost Squad is born.

Chapter Twenty-Nine

RECEIVING MESSAGES

THE NEXT DAY, I'm thinking about our OInK list discussion from last night when I go to see what progress my pumpkins have made. It's only been a few days since I've checked in, but based on the schedule, some of the flowers should have actually started turning to fruit!

Instead, I find the opposite. The whole area looks different, but not in a good way. All the big green leaves on my plants have patchy white spots on them, and their edges are brown. I sink to my knees and move my hand along each vine like I'm checking for a pulse. One after another I see either shriveled, dry blossoms lying on the ground or limp, drooping ones that are barely attached.

"No!!!"

Dad pops his head out of the shed. "What's wrong?"

I don't want to cry over a plant, but right there in the garden, dead pumpkin flowers clutched in my hand, my eyes start to burn. I turn my face away as Dad climbs over the fence. He puts his big hand on my neck and rubs a small circle with his thumb, surveying what's left of the patch.

"It's all ruined," I squeak. "What happened?"

"Well, let's see. Huh." Dad squats down and turns over one of the limp, speckled leaves. "Looks like powdery mildew. It's a disease that loves wet and humid weather like we've had. Sorry, buddy."

Then he picks up a handful of dirt and examines it.

"Whoa. You've got a lot of fertilizer in here too.

Probably too much. Your plants were working too hard to grow, and not hard enough to defend themselves. Next time, go really light with it."

I look around at the flashes of red and yellow already dusting the leaves of the maple trees on the edge of our property. "Next time? It's way too late to start over now!"

This is not how the pumpkin plant cycle is supposed to go. It was very clear on the back of the package. Seed. Sprout. Leaves. Vines. Blossoms. Pumpkins. Not this mess. I pace and flick my hands. I hate that things got messed up in the middle. I wanted to see this through to a big, orange, satisfying, prize-winning conclusion.

"You were really hoping to have something for that contest, weren't you?" Dad asks. I shrug, feeling silly that I ever thought I could win, and for thinking that five hundred dollars would help in the first place.

"But it's more than that, isn't it?" says Dad. "You wanted to finish what you started?"

I nod, relieved he said the words for me.

"Well, I'll tell you what. That's the great thing about gardens: there's always next season. You'll get a do-over!"

"But will there even *be* a garden next summer?" I ask softly.

"Of course! Why wouldn't there be?"

"I mean this *exact* garden, the one right here on Spruce Point?" I stare at the shed. I'm afraid of his answer.

"What . . . ?" he starts. Then he looks at me and knows. "You've heard us talking."

"A little. Some things about the inn, and money. And maybe needing other jobs. And Boston?"

"Ah, Parker. I don't want you to worry about any of that. Mom and I are working on it."

"But I never want to leave here! *This* is where we belong, where the Emertons have always lived!" My voice threatens to open into a Bailey-size wail.

Dad moves in closer and gives me a big hug. "Listen. The important thing is, no matter where we go, and I'm not saying we're going anywhere, we'll always be together. That's it. We could move to the tip-top of Antarctica, and that wouldn't change who we are. You hear me, buddy? We are Emertons, always and forever. Where we live has nothing to do with that. We'll be okay. I promise."

After that, Dad helps me trim off any leaves with the powdery mildew. Which is almost all of them. With each snip of the shears, I feel like I'm cutting off one more tie line keeping us here.

Frankie comes over and calls for us kids at exactly six thirty that evening. We casually walk away from the inn, pretending we're heading down to watch the sunset.

Suddenly Frankie hisses, "Get down!" We all dive behind the storage shed. John and Dev's pickup truck chugs past us and turns left at the end of the lane. As soon as the taillights are out of sight, we get up and run to their cottage.

"We're not going inside," Frankie says. "That's breaking and entering."

"Agree," Sylvie says. "No breaking. Just looking."

John's guitar case is leaning against the deck chair he always sits on to play. We creep up the steps toward it and search the area. For what, I'm not sure.

"Hey!" Bailey says, pointing to the chair. The *Paranormal America: Coastal Maine* book is splayed open, like someone had recently been reading it.

Above us, outside the kitchen window, a homemade driftwood wind chime sways and sounds. The hollow clunking reminds me of the pieces of driftwood that Mrs. Gruvlig has hanging in her tree. I'm about to say something about it to Frankie when a different sound—tires on gravel—sends us skittering around the corner of the cottage and down the deck steps, where we squeeze in behind the cottage's propane tank.

The vehicle's doors open.

"I can't believe I turned around for this." It's Dev's voice. "You need to stop reading that book!"

"Don't worry, it won't take long," we hear John say, followed by the click and swish of the screen door. The cottage windows are open, and their voices get louder as they walk into the living area. Drake giggles and I grip his wrist.

"And it's not like I *really* believe it." John again. "But the book does say that being open to the messages is the only way to receive them. So, let me have my fun and put out my bottles and see if I get any responses. Plus, a lot of the stories seem to happen closer to the time of a new moon, like now. I don't know if we'll be here in another month. This is a one chance deal."

Frankie looks at me and I nod. He's right— we're between the new and first quarter moon now. It'll be getting brighter from here.

There is the sound of clinking and rattling and then footsteps coming outside. A chair scrapes across the deck.

"There," says John.

"Just for fun, right?" says Dev. "I don't need to take you to a doctor to see if the salt air has corroded your brain?"

They laugh and then their voices fade as they return to their truck.

We stay hidden until they drive away again.

"That was close!" whispers Frankie. She waves for us to follow her.

As we head back up the deck stairs, I see something I didn't notice when we were running for cover. It's one of John's guitar picks. I'm sure he left it there accidentally, so I grab it and rub the small, smooth piece of plastic between my fingers.

As we come around the front of the cottage, I see the bottles John has set on the ledge under the driftwood wind chime and I get an idea that makes me laugh. Without thinking too much, I slip the guitar pick into one of them.

Sylvie sees me and covers a giggle with her

hand. Then she takes a piece of sea glass from her pocket and puts it in another bottle.

We take off toward the beach, and when we're all safely on the big rock, burst into loud laughter.

I watched last night until my eyes started to close on their own, but there were no flashes of light. In the morning, Sylvie and I couldn't stay away from our prank scene. We walk with blueberry pails back and forth in the clearing next to John and Dev's cottage, pretending to search for a patch we know is not there.

"Coffee's ready," we hear Dev say through the kitchen window. "Meet me outside."

"You're the best," John answers. "Coming."

With the sound of the door sliding open, we flatten ourselves against the side of the cottage and listen.

"Oh my gosh. John! You're too much. When did you do this?"

"Do what?" asks John, his footsteps joining

Dev's outside. "Oh my gosh, is that my favorite guitar pick? I've been looking everywhere! Where did you find it?"

"I didn't," says Dev.

"Ha ha, very funny," says John. "Ooh, and I see you've given me a sweet piece of blue sea glass too."

"Listen. For real John, I didn't put those there. It was either you or the spirits of those sailors you're always singing about."

"You're a horrible person—you know that, right?" says John.

"I'm not kidding! It wasn't me and you know it."

"Okay, that's how you're gonna play this? Then yeah, sure. I totally believe you. Let's just say it's a good thing you make great coffee."

Their cups clink, and Sylvie and I slip away to report the success of our ghostly prank to the others.

Chapter Thirty

FLOOD ZONE

WHILE I WAIT for Frankie on her front steps the next afternoon, I update the OInK list. I put check marks on numbers two and three, and scratch out number four with an irritated slash.

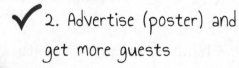

OPERATION INN KEEPERS: OInK

1. Break curse

✓ 2. Advertise (poster) and get more guests

✓ 3. Cooking class—Mom
~~4. ?? Win pumpkin prize money~~
5.

I write the number five on the next line and stare at the blank space, trying to think of other ideas. When nothing comes to mind, my eyes go back to number one. I'm going in circles.

The screen door of the Wilkinses' cottage squeaks open, and Frankie sits down next to me.

"What's up, Buttercup?" she asks.

I bounce my finger on the list. "There aren't enough guests coming, Frankie."

"Hmm, and no pumpkins?" she asks, noticing my scratch mark.

"Pumpkins are off the list. But they were never going to be enough anyway. *None* of the things we've been trying to do will matter if people don't start booking rooms. And summer's nearly over!"

"Hey." She lays a hand on my arm. "It's still

July! There's practically a whole month of summer left. There's plenty of time, Parker."

"Your positivity is exhausting," I say.

"I know. It's a gift." She flicks her hair.

A whistle pierces the air. "C'mon, Adalyn's calling!" says Frankie.

The other kids join us, and we gather under Adalyn's window to read the note she's dropped down for us.

> I wish I could have been part of
> your "ghostly" prank the other night!
> But it gave me an idea that has to
> do with my grandma's tea obsession.
> Details to follow. Also-songs +
> lights = connected? Any updates?

We talk among ourselves to formulate our reply.

"How about this?" asks Sylvie. "The next time John is out playing his guitar, we sneak over and stake out the area. If the songs have something to do with the lights showing up, we need to be right there when he's singing."

"Got it," I say, writing down the instructions for Adalyn.

Frankie rubs her hands together. "The games are on."

Later that night, I'm sitting in bed charting the first quarter moon when I hear the faint sound of John's guitar blowing on the wind. I set down my journal and bolt to the window. I see Frankie signaling to me with her flashlight. And beyond her cottage, a similar blinking from the small opening in Adalyn's curtains. It's time to investigate the presence, or absence, of those odd flashes of green.

Drake and Bailey are fast asleep, but Sylvie slips a long-sleeved T-shirt over her nightgown and we head downstairs. Rather than trying to sneak out, we follow the whir of Mom's mixer to the kitchen, where she's prepping something yummy for breakfast tomorrow.

"What're you two doing up?" she asks when we walk in. Her eyes are red around the rims, and she gives them a quick wipe with the edge of her apron.

"Can't sleep," I say. "You okay?"

"Oh yeah, I just got to thinking about kitchen memories with your Nana, that's all. You guys want a snack?"

"Actually, can we go outside and watch for shooting stars?" Sylvie asks.

Mom gives us a soft smile. "Sure, of course. Gosh, I *love* that your childhoods include such magical experiences." *Outside. Works every time.*

We meet up with Adalyn and Frankie by the row of hemlocks, and then go around the ocean side of the inn so we can cross over the road and hunker down behind Dev's truck. As we approach, we smell the rich woodsmoke from the fire they have going in their firepit. The flames dance, giving the whole area around their cottage a warm glow.

From our hiding spot, we listen. The song John is playing tonight doesn't have words, but I don't need to hear lyrics to know it's a sad one. His fingers pluck at the guitar strings, and it's like he's plucking at my heart too, making it feel full of sorrow for some reason I don't even know. The music mixes with the crackling sounds of the fire.

When the song dwindles to a stop, we hear a few sets of hands clapping.

"Thanks, that's always been one of my favorites when I'm feeling low," I hear Dad say. I didn't realize he was there.

"And you're really out of options?" asks Dev. "The insurance company isn't able to give you any wiggle room?"

"All they do is show me the charts and tell me their hands are tied. With this sea-level rise, practically the entire property is now considered a flood zone. And we have to buy the more expensive coverage in order to keep our mortgage with the bank. It's like a seesaw trying to balance it all.

"But what really worries me is the thought of our main traffic flow being cut off by flooding. The town's fighting with the state about funding for the causeway repairs, but it's not looking good. It'll take a miracle for that money to come through."

"I'm so sorry to hear all this," says John. "It's such a special place. I hope you make it!"

Dad throws a stick into the fire. "Well, thanks. We're not giving up yet! We still have shoulder season. We'll stick it out through that and hope for the best. I wish more people knew how beautiful it is up here in the fall . . ." His voice fades away.

The moon has been in and out of clouds all night, but right now it's clear and bright. Sylvie reaches over and squeezes my hand. I think she's giving me sympathy, but then I see that she's pointing at something. We all peek around the large truck wheel with her and see it: a bright greenish glow. The bottles on John and Dev's windowsill are glimmering with firelight.

But it's not just there. The moon and the fire seem to be playing with the bottles' reflections, tossing around green flashes that ping against the surrounding trees and bushes and onto the crashing ocean waves.

As a wispy cloud passes in front of the moon, the reflections dim. Then in the distance, another spark catches my eye.

"Look," I say, nodding toward Adalyn's house.

Mrs. Gruvlig stands over her own backyard fire circle, her hands raised to the sky, fists shaking.

"Today's the day," Adalyn says. "The anniversary. Of my dad's drowning." Her voice is flat and quiet.

I had thought Mrs. Gruvlig was softening when she started letting Adalyn hang out with us. But now she seems as sad and angry as ever. And that sadness somehow spreads, like smoke from the fire, until it reaches me and I have to run, run,

run across the field, tears cooling my cheeks. I stop at the top of the beach steps.

The girls join me, and we sit sharing our feelings in silence for a while. A loon calls to its mate in the distance.

"I'm sorry your dad is gone," Frankie says to Adalyn, taking her hand.

"And I'm sorry about what we heard earlier, Parker," whispers Sylvie, taking mine.

Then we're all holding hands, and we pass around a squeeze.

"Everything's gonna be okay," says Frankie. "It has to be."

But the reality behind Dad's words washes over me. Nothing we've done this summer has changed anything. Maybe there are no such thing as ghosts, and all these bad things that are happening can be explained logically. But for me, in my gut, the curse is still here, and it's stronger than ever.

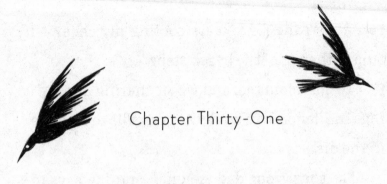

Chapter Thirty-One

SOMETHING SPECIAL

R AIN WASHES OUT the next several weeks. My heart sinks as I flip the calendar to August. Frankie won't be here much longer, and time somehow seems to be moving too fast and too slow.

A few evenings later, the rain finally lets up enough for us to head outside. When it's fully dark, Adalyn bursts from her front door and runs across the field heading to the woods calling "KCM!" We sprint to fall in behind her.

As we pass the bay cottage, Adalyn motions for us to stop. Then she sneaks over to put a few sprigs of sea lavender into John and Dev's glass-bottle collection before continuing to lead us toward the trail.

The ocean sounds loud and angry, stirred up by the weather and the incoming tide. We've missed almost a whole moon cycle to bad weather and August's waning crescent continues to hide behind an overcast sky. There is no firelight or moonglow to reflect off the bottles this time. Just dusky gray all around us.

Until.

A flutter of bright green vibrates just inside the tree line.

My mouth goes dry, but I manage to squeak out, "Curse!"

In that instant, the wavy apparition disappears. But a moment later, another blob of green glows, further down the path. When that one fades, a third shining orb shimmers even deeper in the woods. I can tell by the other kids' faces that I'm not imagining this.

"Run!" yells Frankie, and for a split second I think she means for us to head home, to safety. But she plunges straight into the woods. We sprint behind her.

The thumping sound of our hurried footsteps matches the rhythmic pulsing of blood in my ears as we chase the receding lights. Right when we think we've lost the trail, another flicker beckons, pulling us farther into the darkness.

We're past the tree house now, running through the other side of the woods toward the causeway cove. Wet spruce branches scratch at our faces and arms. I glance back to make sure Bailey is keeping up. She is, with her jaw set and little legs pumping.

"Keep following!" urges Frankie. "They're leading us somewhere, I know it. Don't lose them!"

Nearby, high tide slams against concrete and rocks as we approach the cove. We're all breathing hard, taking ragged gulps of damp, salty air. Drake slips on a rock slick with moss, and I yank him up. We press on, finally pushing through a wall of sharp-barbed bushes and into a clearing.

Around us, the flashes we were chasing blend into a huge pulsing mass that illuminates a handful of gravestones peeking out from the rain-loosened earth, leaning in various directions like teeth that need braces.

"What?" asks Drake in a breathy whisper.

The light's bright core is centered on a worn marker wedged between the roots of a wind-battered spruce. There is a single word etched into the granite.

"Westward!" Frankie exclaims. As soon as she utters the word aloud, a great crashing wave pushes up the hill toward us, soaking our feet and pulling more dirt away from the gravestones. Bailey yelps and I lift her onto my hip.

She buries her face in my neck, but I watch in awe, not blinking once as the green gathers into a spinning vortex that shifts away from us toward the ocean before lifting into the dark sky where it wisps and fades and finally disappears altogether.

A gust of wind swishes through nearby evergreen boughs and I watch as the clouds clear too, almost like they've been pulled away by the mysterious force that moved the green mist. The moon and a wash of stars appear. The fear and adrenaline that had been pumping through me turn to wonder and exhaustion. I set Bailey down, shaking out my arms.

For a moment, we stand in silence. A stillness settles around us as even the wind downshifts and fades.

"What just happened?" asks Drake. "What *was* that?"

I exchange looks with Sylvie and Frankie.

"I . . . but . . . ," Sylvie starts. Then she shakes her head and hugs herself.

"Not a curse," says Frankie looking back to the sky. "I don't think we were meant to be scared."

"Too late!" says Bailey, her voice a crackly whisper. She points to the graveyard. "Are those all dead people?"

I put my hand on her shoulder and squeeze. How have we played near here hundreds of times without ever seeing any of this?

"Where did these come from?" I ask, gently tapping one of the rough stones with my foot.

Sylvie squishes through the churned-up mud next to me and points to a mound of exposed tree roots. "Look how much of this hillside has washed away. They've been buried!"

Frankie brushes off another marker with the side of her sleeve while Drake holds up a flashlight. Most of the words are too faded to read, but she traces her finger on a set of numbers near the bottom. "Whoa. 1743? My dad's history professor friends are going to *freak out*."

"Join the club," says Sylvie, shivering. "This place is creepy!"

"No," I say, stepping to place my hand over the

word *Westward*. "This place is powerful." I understand why we were led here. For the crew, this monument is what my hazelnut tree is to me—something that will always hold space here, even if I have to leave.

"The sailor's spirits haven't been chasing a light or looking for a curse. They *are* the light. They've been looking to be remembered."

"And they chose *us* to get the message," says Frankie. She crosses her hands over her heart.

"Unbelievable," says Sylvie.

"'Cuz we're awesome," says Drake.

"I'm still scared," says Bailey.

That makes me realize maybe the most surprising thing about all of this. Apparently, we've just communicated with the dead. Yet I feel calmer than I have all summer.

Turns out it's not just us and Mr. Wilkins's university buddies who are excited by our find. The next day, soon after Aunt Jenny calls her friends at the historical society, a representative from MOCA—the Maine Old Cemetery Association—comes and declares the spot a site of historic significance. A few days after that, a team of restoration workers arrives. They discover that not only is the monument to the men of the *Westward* there, but also the gravestones of some of the very first non-indigenous people to settle in the area, including Ezekiel Blythe, who our harbor is named after.

We got our picture in the paper, under the headline LOCAL YOUTHS STUMBLE INTO HISTORY. They even came back after dark to take the photo, too, after we'd explained about Adalyn. The article mentioned our last names and the Emerton family's ties to the area, which we all thought was pretty cool.

The man from MOCA was quoted in the article, saying, "The wild and scraggly coastal vegetation had overgrown this spot a long, long time ago. But apparently, all the recent rain combined with the rising tides had degraded the area, washing away enough soil to make the gravestones visible again."

When they interviewed us, we didn't say anything about what had drawn us to the graveyard. We were under oath, after all.

The best part of the whole thing was when a team from the state department of public lands came to see the spot and determined the whole area would be put under *reconstruction protection*, which included building a brand-new retaining wall and a higher causeway bridge.

I never thought I'd see the day when my parents would toast a concrete wall, but that's exactly what happened that night. Nearly everyone from the peninsula had gathered at the inn to celebrate, and a bunch of people from town, too. Even us kids got in on it, sloshing grape juice as we clinked glasses.

There was only one person missing. One person who was still the same, acting as if nothing had changed.

Mrs. Gruvlig.

Chapter Thirty-Two

GHOSTLY

AT THE END of the week, Mom's serving coffee and fresh scones on the porch for the inn and cottage guests on the final day of the summer season.

Earlier, I'd passed the mud-caked boots of an overnighter who had gone on a hike yesterday. On a whim, I took them with me down to the beach where I'd gone to watch the sunrise. I'd clapped the dusty soles together and swirled the treads clean in a shallow tide pool, hurrying back to place them exactly where they'd been before anyone else woke up.

Now I struggle to hide my smile as the woman thanks Mom for taking care of her filthy hiking gear.

"I'm glad your boots got cleaned, but it honestly wasn't me," Mom responds with genuine confusion.

"Ah, must have been the fairies," the woman says, winking as she fiddles with her big butterfly earrings. "I'll bet there's tons of them flitting about these magical woods."

"Or ghosts," says John. "I've been reading a lot about spirits lately, and I think there are some friendly ones playing around on this peninsula!"

His eyes are serious. Frankie stuffs a scone into her mouth and nearly chokes on her laughter.

Mom has planned a special goodbye dinner later that day for the Wilkinses and John and Dev, who are also leaving. John says his research is done, and it's time for them to move up the coast, following the sailors' songs into Canada.

Mom hasn't let anyone into the kitchen since after breakfast, and the whole house smells amazing. She told us the menu would be based in part on things she learned doing a joint cooking class with Dev a few weeks earlier called *Spicy Seafood Sampler*. That had been a huge hit, and even led to Dev getting a call from the *Harbor Herald* to ask if he would share his Mussels Masala recipe for an insert about unique ways to prepare local foods.

When Mom opens the doors to the dining room and calls us all in, she surprises everyone by presenting a full Indian dinner—starting, of course, with the mussels.

"Mrs. Emerton, you are a prize pupil," says Dev, eyes closed as he savors his first bite.

"And you are a wonderful teacher," says Mom. Then Dad asks Dev how they say *cheers* in India.

Dev laughs, telling us he had asked the same thing on his trip there.

"It's *cheers*, same as here." We all clink glasses.

After dinner, John calls Frankie and me out onto the porch.

"I wanted to give you your book back," he says. "I hope you kids will keep watching for unusual activity after I'm gone. Because I'm pretty sure there really is something extraordinary going on around here." Frankie hides her smile behind her hand, and I practice my innocent eyes.

"Mr. John, will you play one more concert before you go?" begs Bailey, coming out to join us. She tilts her head and paws at the cat ears on her headband with curled hands. "Meow?"

"How can I say no to such a majestic feline?" he asks.

"I'll go get your guitar!" I dash to grab it and rush back before he can change his mind.

"Sadly, this one's about leaving," says John. And he starts to play.

I thought I heard the Old Man say:

"Leave her, Johnny, leave her."

Tomorrow you will get your pay,

And it's time for us to leave her.

Leave her, Johnny, leave her!

Oh, leave her, Johnny, leave her!

For the voyage is long and the winds

don't blow

And it's time for us to leave her.

Oh, the wind was foul and the sea

ran high.

"Leave her, Johnny, leave her!"

She shipped it green and none went by.

And it's time for us to leave her.

Leave her, Johnny, leave her!

Oh, leave her, Johnny, leave her!

But now we're through, so we'll go on

shore.

And it's time for us to leave her.
Leave her, Johnny, leave her!
Oh, leave her, Johnny, leave her!
For the voyage is long and the winds
don't blow
And it's time for us to leave her.

He nods his head to our applause, and we all crowd in for goodbye hugs. John's buttoning up his guitar case when we hear a noise that we've never heard before.

It's Mrs. Gruvlig, out in her front yard. Laughing. Head back, from the belly, loud and honking. We scramble over to Frankie's porch to see what's going on.

Adalyn finally figured out how to prank her grandma. Mrs. Gruvlig is looking down at a sign that says FRESH TEA. Surrounding the sign are dozens of teaspoons sticking out of the dirt, tea bags attached to each of them with rubber bands.

"Huh," says Frankie, sitting back on her heels. "Miracles *do* happen!"

It does seem miraculous, hearing laughter from Mrs. Gruvlig. And if something like that can happen, maybe there's a chance for other miracles too. Like: a small inn on the coast of Maine becomes wildly popular, and a boy gets to live there happily ever after, the end.

That night at Adalyn time we hear a whistled *K-C-M* Morse code from the dock, and hurry to join her. Mom even lets Bailey go, making her promise to stay right next to Sylvie the whole time, preferably holding her hand.

The ocean is calm, and the gentle waves lap tongues of water over a line of dark seaweed on the shore, pulling some back toward the ocean each time they retreat. The streak of moonlight on the water points right at us.

"I can't believe I have to leave tomorrow!" Frankie takes off her sneakers and dangles her feet. "I wish the Peninsula Fair wasn't always literally the week my dad has to be back at the university. I hate missing it!"

"How do you think I'll feel?" says Adalyn. "I'll be close enough to smell it, but I won't be able to go either."

"Why not?" asks Bailey. Then she frowns. "Oh, right . . . daytime."

I throw a big rock, *kaplunk*, into the water. "Sorry, Adalyn."

"It's okay. I'm getting used to it. Sort of. But guess what?" She sits up. "I have great news!"

"They found a number bigger than infinity?" asks Bailey.

"Chocolate grows on trees?" asks Drake.

"Shhh . . . ," I say.

"Actually, chocolate does grow on trees, technically," says Sylvie.

"Guys! My news?" Adalyn holds her hand out to stop them.

"Sorry, yes, tell it!" says Frankie.

"My mom got a job at the hospital in Portland! We're going to move up here to Maine, permanently!"

"Yay!" Sylvie gives her a side hug. "That's not that far. You could come here on weekends!"

"You're so lucky," says Frankie. "I'm jealous!"

"And I'm jealous of both of you," I say. "At least you know where you'll be in the fall."

"There's still time for things to turn around, Parker," says Sylvie. "My mom said she's never had a bigger client than the inn these past weeks because of all the extra stuff going on."

"And there've been more people in and out lately, right?" asks Drake.

"I know there've been some good things. But I still hear Mom and Dad talking a lot about 'plan B.' Yesterday they were on the porch and Dad brought up Boston again." I pick at some barnacles crusted on the side of the dock.

"Is that what *plan B* stands for?" asks Bailey. "Boston?"

"*Plan B* means the thing you have to do when you don't get what you really want," says Sylvie.

"*Plan B* means selling the inn and not living here," I say. Bailey leans tight against my side.

"That would be the worst," says Drake.

We sit in silence. I feel like I'm being pulled down through swirling darkness, like the rock I tossed into the ocean.

"You know, whatever happens, I'll always be glad I met you guys," says Adalyn. "After I got diagnosed and had to move, I was worried I'd never make friends again. But then look!" She sweeps her hand around at all of us. "Moving isn't always *so* awful." Then her eyes droop down, and she pushes her finger into a knot in the wood. "But I really hope you don't have to go."

"Ditto," I say.

"Ditto," says everyone else, in a line like an echo.

"And I hope you don't forget about me when I leave for Portland!" says Adalyn.

"Or me either!" says Frankie. "New York is three times farther away!"

"Never!" says Sylvie. "We swear on the oath of the KCM."

"Friends to the end," I say, putting my hand in the middle. Then everyone stacks their hands on mine—two, three, four, five, six. I like the weight of it. Heavy, solid, secure.

Chapter Thirty-Three

FAMOUS

THE NEXT MORNING is fog-covered and chilly. I wake up before all the other kids and find Dad in the kitchen, staring out the window. I puzzle-piece against him and he hugs me close.

"The summer ends as it began," he says. "We'll have the place to ourselves again soon." His face is tight, and he's chewing on his lip.

"And it's pretty great that we won't have to worry anymore about the causeway flooding and being closed off, right?" I hate seeing him worried.

"Sure, that's very true. The road will be fixed. But the trick remains getting enough people to come across it."

We're finishing up breakfast when Frankie bangs in through the back door, waving something in the air.

"Mrs. Emerton! Mr. Emerton! Check it out! You're famous!"

"What are you talking about?" asks Mom, wiping her hands on a kitchen towel.

"Look!" She hands over a copy of *Coastal Traditions* magazine. "Deb just picked it up on her last run to the post office!"

"We're on the front cover!" I shout, peeking over Mom's shoulder. It's a beautiful picture of the inn, with the sun sparkling off the ocean behind it.

"Oh, wow!" says Dad.

"*The Home Away Inn—A Hidden Gem for Ghosts and Other Guests*, by John Stevens. Oh my goodness!" says Mom.

We all crowd around while Mom reads John's article out loud.

Away from the crowds, away from the worries of everyday life, sits a welcoming inn and four sturdy cottages. The Home Away Inn near Blythe Harbor, Maine, is indeed the high point of the Spruce Point peninsula, as promised in their advertisement I happened upon when I stopped for a lobster roll at the nearby Swirl Top Ice Cream Shop in town.

I decided to check it out and am so glad I did. While researching the rich history of local sea shanties, I discovered something else equally as wonderful: a community of people who treated me and my traveling companion as friends and were as eager to learn our traditions as they were to share theirs.

Do not miss chef and co-owner Sarah Emerton's highly regarded cooking classes, which leave students full of knowledge and delicious food. Her Saturday night buffets are newly open to locals as well as inn guests, and feature some of the most authentic coastal recipes and decadent desserts I've ever tasted.

From the sun-kissed beach mornings to the cool evening breezes, the location of the Home Away Inn is spectacular. Once you check in, you will not want to leave. And apparently, some former guests may have taken this feeling to heart, as there were many times that a ghostly presence was felt on the property.

Watch closely for small, dark shapes moving about in the night, long after most children have gone to bed. And if you're open to receiving the messages, lost items and gifts may come your way. But rest assured, if there are indeed spirits on the grounds, they are quite friendly, and will only add to the amazing experience that awaits you at your new Home Away from home.

But act fast and make your reservation now, because the treasures of the inn may soon become a thing of the past. Struggling with the effects of our sluggish economy, owners Paul and Sarah Emerton were honest about the realities of running such a large waterfront property.

"This place has been in my family for generations," said Paul, while his wife Sarah added, "We'd like to be here forever, but you can't live on the scent of salt water alone."

For all our sakes, I hope the Home Away Inn stays open for generations to come.

"This is amazing!" says Dad, sweeping Mom up off the floor in a big hug. "We're famous!"

"*Coastal Traditions!*" says Mom. "Everyone reads this magazine! I'm calling Jenny right now!"

Frankie grabs my arm and points to the woods. She always says goodbye to the fort and the ocean one last time. We run across the field, knocking into each other and then spinning away, like bowling pins after the ball hits. When we get to the fort, we celebrate with a Frankenparker, hollering, "Hip-hip, elbow-elbow, head-shoulders-knees-toes-POP!"

"You know, if Adalyn stays up here, you guys will be year-round friends. You'll have so much fun you won't even miss me." Frankie walks around the edges of the tree house, running her hands across each surface.

"That's the dumbest thing I've ever heard," I say, pulling on her elbow so she's facing me. "Adalyn's cool and all, but it's not the same as you being here. I wish you never had to go."

"Parker, let's make a pact."

"Is this gonna involve blood?" I ask, pulling my hand away. I've never forgotten the time Frankie wanted us to become blood siblings.

"No," she laughs. "Let's just agree to always be friends. No matter what."

"Even if I have to move to some dumb small house in Boston?" I ask.

"Sure—you'd be closer to me then!"

"Even if I grow warts all over me?"

"Sure—I've always liked frogs. Some of them turn into princes."

"But that's only if . . . Oh." My face flushes.

"I'm not saying *that*!" Frankie shoves me.

I laugh and raise my right hand. "I, Parker Emerton, do solemnly swear that I will never stop being friends with Frankie Wilkins."

She grabs my shoulders, and for a quick moment we stare at each other. "Good," she says. "And if you break that oath, I will haunt you." Then she zips down the ladder and back up the trail, headed to the ocean.

I follow and when we get to the dock, we collapse side by side on the warm wooden planks. My heart finally slows down to match the gentle tug of the waves against the beams beneath us. A kayaker glides silently along the shore.

"*Create file*," says Frankie. "*Save as.*"

"What?"

"I'm uploading mental pictures."

I study Frankie's profile. "You're strange."

"Thank you."

We both stare out at the bay. Mrs. Wilkins calls for Frankie, and we hear the thud of the hatchback on her dad's wagon.

"I hate goodbye day." I fling a stone as far as I can, watching its ripples spread.

"Me too," says Frankie, shifting to face me. "When I'm older, I'm never going to leave Maine. I think I'll be like John and spend my time traveling up and down the coast, researching interesting things."

"And I'll be right here, running the inn. Like my family before me." My voice fails me with a squeak, and I look down, embarrassed.

"Don't worry," says Frankie, tapping her hand

lightly on my back. "You will be here. And I'll be your best guest."

"You're already our best guest," I say. "And my best friend."

"Same," she says. She stands up and grabs my hand, pulling me to my feet. "Grown-ups—never!" she shouts over the rolling water.

Then we both lean forward into the wind and yell a promise.

"Kids—forever!"

Chapter Thirty-Four

THE GHOST OF SPRUCE POINT

ONE WEEK LATER, Dad wakes me up in the middle of the night. I look at the numbers glowing on my clock: 11:30 p.m.

"Time to go," he whispers. I join Bailey in the back seat of the chilly car.

"Ready?" says Mom, turning around to us.

"To the fair!" says Bailey. She's bouncing like it's Christmas morning.

As we ride along, the moon follows us, lighting up the red- and yellow-tipped leaves of the maple trees along the road. And it's not just any moon. It's the big bright last full moon of the summer. It's not as rare or special as a super blood moon or even a blue moon, but it does feel like a good sign.

When we pull up, Mrs. Gruvlig and Adalyn are waiting for us. A lot of vendors are already there too, a full nine hours before the grand opening. The half-lit surroundings give the fairgrounds an eerie, magical glow.

"I still can't believe you did this for me!" Adalyn says.

"Well, I may have asked a few favors," says Dad, "but once people found out who you were, and made the connection to your dad, they all started offering to help. A lot of people around here loved Pete. Your grandma most of all, of course." He reaches to pat Mrs. Gruvlig's shoulder, and she lets him.

"I had no idea . . . so many people . . ." Mrs. Gruvlig doesn't seem to know what to say. Dad saves her by clearing his throat and making an announcement.

"Hear ye! The first ever Peninsula *Moon* Fair is open for business! Miss Adalyn, it's all yours!" Dad bows low and points the way through the turnstiles.

Adalyn takes off running, and Bailey and I chase after her. I've never been out of the house this late, and I've never been on so many rides without waiting in line before. It's awesome. In between, we play the two carnival games that opened for us. Mom even pulls out some packaged cotton candy so we can "taste the fair" too. We shout *echo* into the darkened animal pavilion and jump when a cow moos back. Adalyn digs her hands into a box of blue ribbons that will be awarded over the weekend.

"First place, *me!*" she shouts, holding fistfuls in the air.

The grown-ups trail along behind us, holding our stuffed-animal prizes and cups of soda as we climb on one last ride. We whip past them, our tilt-a-whirl car jerking as it dips and spins, and they grin and wave each time.

"I've never seen your grandma smile so much," I say, wobbling my way down the exit ramp.

"Me neither. She looks . . . happy. The phone has been ringing so much the past few weeks. And she's actually been answering it—and talking to people!"

I reflect her grin and stop for a moment to take in our temporary kingdom. The lights of the rides are clicking off, one by one. Everyone's going back to their homes or trailers to get some sleep before they reopen for real in the bright light of day.

"I don't want tonight to be over!" says Adalyn.

"It's not quite yet," says Dad. "Follow me."

We head to the far side of the fairgrounds and Dad leads us down a trail I've never noticed before, into the nearby woods. A short way down the path, a small brook is blocked up by some rocks, forming a swimming hole. The moonlight reflects off the water like a giant night-light. We all take our shoes off and put our tired feet in, even Mrs. Gruvlig.

"Your dad and I used to come here all the time," Dad says to Adalyn. "We'd stick our little homemade fishing poles in and never catch a thing. But we also never got bored. Your dad made everything fun."

As we listen to Dad and Mrs. Gruvlig tell Pete stories, Bailey curls up and falls asleep on Mom's lap. Adalyn and I gather and stack rocks, biggest to smallest, all along the edge of the pool.

After a while, the moon dips down behind the trees, marking how much time has passed.

"Okay, gang, we'd better call it," says Dad. "We'll get you home to your journal while the moon is still up, Parker."

"It's all right, Dad," I say. "It can wait. I know it'll be back in the sky again tomorrow." Dad looks at Mom and the two come over to squish me in a hug.

We slip our shoes on and head back through the fairgrounds. The sky is shifting from black to gray as we weave through the metal skeletons of the rides on our way to the parking lot.

"You'll come for tea Friday," Mom says, putting a hand on Mrs. Gruvlig's arm before we part ways.

The older woman pauses, her chin tucked to the side as if she wants to say both *yes* and *no*.

"I'll bring crab cakes," she says, her voice gruff as she turns abruptly toward her car, pulling Adalyn along behind her.

We wave goodbye to them and watch their small rusty Volvo putt away. A few faint stars still cling to the sky.

"Wishing stars," mumbles Bailey, lifting her head off Mom's shoulder.

"I don't know what I'd even wish for after a night like tonight," says Mom, nuzzling Bailey's hair as she lowers her into the car.

"I do. I wish for a puppy," says Bailey. "And a mountain of cotton candy."

"You already *had* a mountain of cotton candy," says Dad.

"Actually, I change my mind. I do know what my wish is," says Mom, turning around to Bailey and me as we buckle into the back seat. "I wish for you kids to always know that no matter what happens, you're the most important things in the world to Dad and me. You're our blue ribbons."

"I second that wish!" says Dad. "We're double prizewinners!"

On the drive home, I put my window down and get a waft of low tide as the air rushes past. A thin band of light grows along the horizon. Just above it, an unmistakable shimmer of green pulses then flits off in the direction of the ocean. I squeeze my eyes shut and when I open them again, it's gone. I don't ask if anyone else saw. I'm not afraid anymore.

Bailey leans her head against my shoulder. Dad is singing along to the radio. I close my eyes and whisper, "*Save as* . . ."

"What's all this?" asks Dad as we turn off the main road onto our lane.

"Who are all those people?" asks Bailey, sitting up tall to see.

"And what are they doing here so early?" asks Mom. Our driveway is lined with cars, at least six of them. One of them looks like a hearse. As we pull closer, we can see that the first three are identical. Sleek and black, with tinted windows and gold lettering on the side: *Ghost Hunters International.*

"Ghost Hunters International?" Mom says. "What the heck is that?"

"It's a TV show!" I shout. "I saw it when we stayed in that hotel room with cable!"

"TV show!?" says Bailey. "Are we gonna be famous again?"

Mom doesn't seem happy. "I don't want them trespassing here, Paul. Kids, stay in the car."

Dad pulls up in front of the inn, and he and Mom get out to talk to the man and woman who are on the porch, knocking on the door. It seems like there are people everywhere, walking around the cottages, going down toward the dock, or just sitting in their cars.

Mom and Dad talk to the two strangers for a long time. I lean my upper body out of the car window and strain to hear what they're saying, but they're too far away. Finally Mom calls and waves us over. Dad is shaking hands with the lady.

"Bailey, Parker," says Mom, "this is Mr. Drew and Ms. Foster. They heard there might be something unique about our inn, and they're going to be staying for a while to have a look around."

"And their whole crew, too," says Dad. "So, let's make them feel welcome." He's speaking calmly, but I can tell by his eyes that he's dancing inside.

"Are you here because of the ghost?" asks Bailey. I bite the inside of my cheek. She could blow this whole thing for us right now.

"Well, we hope so," says Mr. Drew, kneeling down. "What can you tell us about it?"

"It's not an *it*, it's a she. And she's real."

"That's exactly what we're hoping," says Ms. Foster, rubbing her hands together.

"Everybody, start unloading! We're staying!" yells Mr. Drew.

That evening, when the visitors are settled into the cottages and guest rooms, we all gather for a first-ever *Welcome Fall* feast. Mom pours cider for everyone, and I tap on the side of my cup with a fork until the room quiets down. Dad smiles at me, then nods.

"A toast," I say, raising my glass. "To ghosts!"

Acknowledgments

*"There's a winding lane on the coast of
Maine that's wound around my heart."*
—Hal Lone Pine

Thank you to my parents, John and Carol Merrifield, for following the call of adventure that led to
a winding lane on the coast of Maine over twenty
years ago. And even though they'll always be *from
away*, thanks also to the Blue Hill community for
welcoming them, and by extension their kids and
grandkids, to the area. Mom, you have sprinkled
magic on so many lives and childhoods. We are
all so lucky that you like to celebrate good times
(come on). Dad, we miss you and we thank you for

always saying yes when we begged for *one more song.*

I am grateful to the Merrifield grandchildren: Maggie, Nellie, Isabelle, Celia, Kate, and Vijay. All my memories of summers at Treetops are infused with your cousin capers, skits, shenanigans, and sweetness, all of which helped steer the emotion of this story. And to my own cousins: Wilson, Sue, Todd, Craig, and Teddy, and my siblings Jenny and David—thank you for being my first friends.

Boatloads of gratitude to Alyson Heller, an editor with a big heart and true talent. Thank you for keeping my compass pointed in the right direction, and for welcoming Parker and me to Aladdin, where we've been stretched, guided, and encouraged to be our best selves.

And to the whole team at Aladdin, who made this story shine and sing and kept me away from rogue waves, including copyeditor Jen Strada, proofreader Stacey Sakal, production editor Olivia Ritchie, as well as designer Tiara Iandiorio. Kristina Kister, thank you for the amazing cover art and for bringing the magic of Spruce Point to life.

I am so fortunate to have ended up in the safe harbor that is Prospect Agency. Thank you, Emma Sector, for your sharp editorial eye, your kindness, and your dogged pursuit of what was best for me and my work when I had the pleasure of being under your wing. Charlotte Wenger, thank you for spinning a strong, safe web for me to land in when the time was right. I am grateful!

Thank you to the Connecticut Shoreline Alliance/Tassy Walden Awards committee for your continued support of new voices in children's literature. The early acknowledgment that this project had promise was instrumental in me seeing it through to "the end."

I'm grateful to Melzen Farm Supply for sponsoring and hosting the spring 2015 Glastonbury Greatest Pumpkin Program. I had a lot to learn and a small pumpkin to show for it. I also had a lot of fun. Thanks also to students at Salisbury Central School in Lakeville, CT, who welcomed me on career day years ago and helped me brainstorm things that were creepy. Likewise, Mrs. Rhoades's fifth graders at Hebron Avenue School in Glastonbury, CT, could always be counted on when I needed kid feedback. Thank you!

Critique group is a harsh name for a place where I've always found such love and encouragement. The Glastonbury SCBWI critique group gave me a monthly place to go and claim my identity as a writer. The Red Barn Writers are a guiding constellation of incredibly talented people who marched through multiple drafts of this story with me until it was ready to leave the barn. Thank you Holly Howley, Jill Dailey, Paula Wilson, Jessica Loupos, Kristina O'Leary, and Michele Manning for holding space for me when my courage gave out, and for following me to Maine in the winter! And to the Fab Four, thanks for always pushing me to keep moving forward. Holly Howley, Jeanne Zulick Ferruolo, and Eileen Washburn, there's no one else I'd rather be a non-blonde with! Eileen, thank you for the early read and feedback that helped steer this wayward dinghy.

Other early readers whose close attention strengthened this story include Tonia Branson and Angie Bell. Tonia, thank you for accidentally printing out the manuscript in book form and helping me manifest my dream. Angie, thank you for understanding the heart underneath it all, and for being my blow-up-hot-dog ride or die.

Thanks always to dear family for your continued support: Tandons, Holdens, Hamms, Garlands, Merrifields, Bowens—I've loved adventuring through life with all of you.

Special thanks to Charlie and Harper Tandon and Celia (the other one!) and Clancy Chittenden for reminding me that the magic of childhood never ends, it only grows stronger when fueled by the next generation's imaginations.

An ocean-full of gratitude and love to Kate and Vijay, for giving me the gift of reliving childhood through your eyes. Being your mom has been the greatest blessing of my life. I know you are paddling your kayaks further out into deep water now, but I'm confident you have all the strength you need to make it around the island. I'm proud of you.

And finally, to my dear Mr. Half-Empty, Rajnish. It's your wind that fills my sails. Thank you for climbing up Blue Hill and asking me that important question at the top. I'm so grateful for all the years of happy trails that have followed. Te amo.